**Prisoners Bound
for Another Planet**

Yukako Kabei
Illustrated by: Shuns

And I learned something big. It seems that before my grandmother in Easterbury took me in, I was on a ship with my mother. But my mother was with an Undying man, and the Church Soldiers that were after them got them. . . .

Becca, if you meet my mother, tell her that I'm doing okay. Because I'm not alone now.

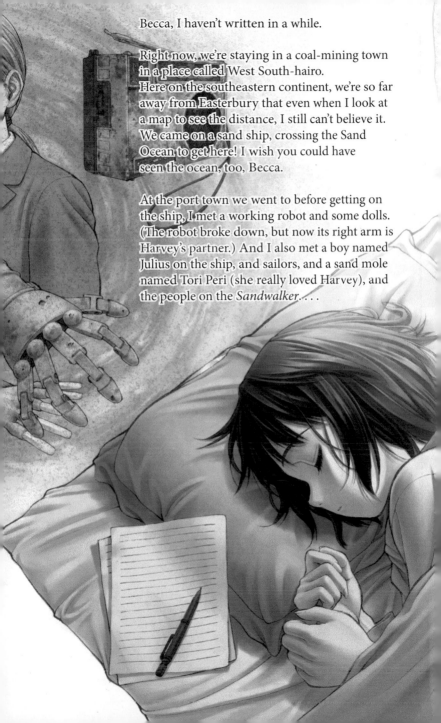

Becca, I haven't written in a while.

Right now, we're staying in a coal-mining town in a place called West South-hairo. Here on the southeastern continent, we're so far away from Easterbury that even when I look at a map to see the distance, I still can't believe it. We came on a sand ship, crossing the Sand Ocean to get here! I wish you could have seen the ocean, too, Becca.

At the port town we went to before getting on the ship, I met a working robot and some dolls. (The robot broke down, but now its right arm is Harvey's partner.) And I also met a boy named Julius on the ship, and sailors, and a sand mole named Tori Peri (she really loved Harvey), and the people on the *Sandwalker*....

# KIELI

## Prisoners Bound for Another Planet

Yen
Press

KIELI: Prisoners Bound for Another Planet
YUKAKO KABEI

Translation: Alethea Nibley and Athena Nibley
Additional Translation and Adaptation: Sarah Alys Lindholm

Yen Press
Hachette Book Group
237 Park Avenue, New York, NY 10017

Visit our Web sites at www.HachetteBookGroup.com and www.YenPress.com.

Yen Press is an imprint of Hachette Book Group, Inc. The Yen Press name and logo are
trademarks of Hachette Book Group, Inc.

First Yen Press Edition: September 2010

Library of Congress Cataloging-in-Publication Data

Kabei, Yukako.
    [Hoshi e yuku shuujintachi. English]
    Prisoners bound for another planet / Yukako Kabei ; [illustrated by Shunsuke Taue ;
translation, Alethea Nibley and Athena Nibley]. —1st Yen Press ed.
        p. cm. —(Kieli ; v. 3)
    Summary: Kieli and Harvey have settled down in a mining town in South–Hairo, where
Kieli works at a diner while Harvey stays at home, but his mysterious disappearances to
take care of business lead her to an unwelcome discovery.
    ISBN 978-0-7595-2931-1
    [1. Fantasy.]  I. Taue, Shunsuke, ill.  II. Nibley, Alethea.  III. Nibley,
Athena.  IV. Title.
    PZ7.K1142Pri 2010
    [Fic]—dc22

                                                              2010001934

10  9  8  7  6  5  4  3  2  1

RRD-C

Printed in the United States of America

PRISONERS BOUND FOR ANOTHER PLANET

A long, long time ago, before mankind had a way to traverse the stars and lived all packed together on one cramped planet, there was something called the "death penalty." Apparently, they would cover a prisoner's head with a cloth, sit him in a chair, and choose a lucky candidate from a group of volunteers to be the executioner, who would flip a switch that sent a high-voltage current shooting from the top of the prisoner's head to the tips of his toes.

On a whim, he talked to one of the prisoners about this while doing his last patrol before turning on the deep-freeze capsules. The prisoner thought about it for a while, and then said, "I like that. It's a really fair system and doesn't make for any future troubles."

*I see.* Come to think of it, strangely, he thought the man might be right.

These days, they froze prisoners with life sentences and sent them to remote regions of space. The prisoners were worked like dogs until they died on the newly settled planets.

And the crew members of the convoy ships that took them there—well, their circumstances weren't much different. They went into deep freeze and journeyed across space for decades; and not only that, while they were hopping across the surface of time on their light-speed cruise, centuries passed by on the ground, so the astronauts were completely shot out of the flow of society. It really wasn't a very upstanding profession.

"Royal straight flush. Federation army," his colleague said from the other side of the game board, spreading out his hand to show him.

"How the—?" he couldn't help calling out in bewilderment. Looking at the other man's cards, he saw that he had skillfully gathered the five picture cards of the federation army suit: judge, sword, revolution, bishop's staff, and shepherd.

"Liar! No one gets a royal straight flush just like that! You cheated!"

"Sorry, but it's skill."

"Then let's see you do it again. One more hand."

"It's almost time. We have to get ready to go into cold sleep."

"Damn it, winning and running…"

*He could at least let me enjoy winning the last hand; he's got no consideration.* Cursing bitterly to himself, he reluctantly cleaned up the cards and game board. *The next time I play with these cards will be decades from now; I hope I don't get rusty during the long cold sleep.* (He figured his colleague would say, "You're not that good anyway," but no one was asking him.)

He casually gazed outside the special quarter-sphere-shaped glass projecting out in front of the flight deck.

It was an ocean of pitch-black, as far as the eye could see. A cruel environment with no air or water, or even the slightest sound—instead, rays of space radiation flew past each other. But their forebears set out on a whim on a long, long adventure, believing that somewhere in this expanse, there must be solid ground they could land on.

Even if it was a run-down planet, with only a barren wilderness and meager energy resources, the children born there would take root, build cities, and hand down a new planet's history—but such poetic thoughts weren't his own; he got them from his colleague.

When he woke up from deep freeze, he would likely be able

to gaze through that glass onto a sand-colored planet, wrapped in a hazy atmosphere.

"Hmm?" He happened to glance down and see that his colleague had taken the "exile" picture card from the deck and was sticking it to the dashboard.

"What are you doing?"

"For good luck. So we arrive safely," he answered, shrugging lightly in his sky-blue work clothes, then made a prayerlike gesture to the exile on the card.

...*Damn, this guy likes showing off.*

"I'm going on down, you sentimental sap. I'll take sleep over praying."

He left his colleague behind and slid down the connector pipe from the flight deck to the middeck's capsule room.

Now, a little nap before the exile planet in remote space...

# CHAPTER 1

## AT THE VERY TOP OF THE SLOPE

"Um, it's my birthday...."

Harvey wondered what expression he must have worn when she started talking timidly that morning. If he were to make a comparison, he figured it was probably something like the face you'd make hearing some alien language from the edge of space while wondering, "What the hell is she saying?" That's just how estranged he was from that word. He didn't even remember if he had a birthday, and if he did, it would just make him feel empty, so he didn't want to think about it.

He turned these thoughts over in a distant corner of his mind as he gazed into her black eyes for about five seconds, and then answered, "Oh, I see."

He knew his reaction was lacking somehow. "Oh, do you want something?" he tried again, but that wasn't quite right either. Wasn't there something you were supposed to say before you got to such a materialistic question?

"No. I don't need anything." He thought she would get depressed or start sulking or something, but, unexpectedly, she answered as if it didn't really bother her that much. Just as he'd come to expect each morning, she briskly readied herself to go out; finally she pulled the radio's cord over her head and said, "But it would be nice if you were home tonight."

"...If that's what you want."

"Promise. No matter what," she emphasized, so he couldn't help responding, "Yes, ma'am."

She smiled happily. "Well, I'm off, then!" She spun around and cheerfully left the dining area.

He heard the door open and close on the other side of the mere token of a hallway that led from the dining room, and her nimble footsteps went farther and farther down the hall outside.

*Sigh…*

The exchange reminded Harvey of just how easy life had gotten, and he felt oddly uncomfortable; he turned around on the sofa and rested his chin on its back. The springs creaked slightly underneath him. The somewhat seasoned sofa had been pushed under the window overlooking the street below, and lately that had become his established spot.

The sofa for two, a rusty dining table, and a tiny storage shelf that had been there before they moved in were all that fit in the combined living, dining, and kitchen area of the commonplace, cheap apartment that also included a bedroom, a bathroom, and a short hall. It had been almost one month since they'd started renting a room on the third floor of this five-story, iron-framed building that looked out on the squalid hill road that overflowed with a sense of liveliness.

Living in an apartment. He got the feeling it was ridiculously unlike him, and he wanted to laugh.

*What am I doing…?*

The chilly but pleasant air of the early-spring morning came in through the open window. He shifted his gaze through it and saw Kieli hop down from the outdoor staircase on the side of the building. As soon as she got out onto the street, she turned at a right angle and passed under the window.

As he casually watched her go, he realized (after thinking for a while) that if it was her birthday, she must be fifteen now. Maybe it was because he saw her every day, but he didn't feel as if she had changed at all; if he had to find something different, it would be that her short hair had grown just a little, and her clothes had gotten somewhat more mature. A spring blouse, cropped pants, sandals—no, he was just imagining it. The clothes proved only that it really was spring.

"It's just…," he muttered, not knowing himself what it "just" was, and let his gaze wander to the sky diagonally above him. Just then, a long, narrow shadow fell before his eyes.

A fork.

The kind used for eating, of course.

Harvey reached out instinctively, and nearly slipped and fell as he leaned out the window frame and caught it just in the nick of time. He snatched it without thinking, so normally the fork's tines would have stabbed his hand; but fortunately, he had reached out with his prosthetic right arm, so all the tines did was create a dry, metallic sound.

"Nice…"

He breathed a sigh of relief, grateful for both his own reflexes and those of his false arm, and, still hanging limply out the window, he looked down at the street below to see Kieli pattering by directly below him.

He watched her go, then craned his neck to glare at the floor above.

He could make out a short silhouette in the window two floors up, but the instant he thought their eyes met, it disappeared.

*They're upgrading their weaponry.…*

Two days ago, a paper airplane; yesterday, a glass marble; and today, a fork. It was looking as though tomorrow it would be a meat cleaver or a wall clock. At this point, he couldn't let them keep doing whatever the hell they wanted anymore.

"Good morning."

As soon as he climbed the outside stairway to the fifth floor

and stepped onto the walkway, a man who seemed to be a resident of the floor greeted him. Harvey had a habit of walking
around at times when he wouldn't run into too many people;
so although he was meeting this man for the first time, having
no intention of bothering with anything like neighborly rela-
tions, he ignored the man and kept walking past him. (He did
have some idea that his manners had gotten incredibly bad
lately.)

The resident shrugged and went down the stairs.

Harvey watched him go out of the corner of his eye, then
faced front again. A narrow walkway, built exactly the same
way as the one on the third floor, led inside. When he looked
forward, doors lined a concrete wall on his right, and the
wall of the building behind them stuck to the left of the
hallway so closely that there was almost no space between
them. He didn't know which building had been built first, but
either way, he was impressed with however they managed to
do it.

He stood in front of the door equivalent to theirs on the
third floor and started to ring the bell beside it but stopped.
He didn't really have any reason to bother with civility. He
noticed that the doorknob was rusty, and there was a light
layer of dust over it.

When he reached for it, the man from before popped out
from the corner of the stairway. "You want to rent that apartment?"

"No..."

"That place is trouble. You'd better forget about it," the man
rattled on one-sidedly, wearing an expression as if something
had given him chills, and didn't give Harvey a chance to

answer. "No one's lived there for two years. There's no one there, but you can still hear sounds and voices....I'm not lying. I live next door. But the landlord'll tell you that no one will rent it because I keep putting ideas in people's heads. Ah, if he sees me here, I'll be in trouble again."

He looked around, as if the landlord actually frightened him more than the eerie phenomenon, and with a hurried "Later," he disappeared down the stairs in a panic.

"......"

*I guess it takes all kinds in this world,* Harvey found himself thinking.

Once the footsteps disappeared down the stairs, he looked around to double-check that he was alone and then slowly turned the knob. The apartment was unlocked. He pulled on the door and heard a light, rusty sound and saw dust scraping across the floor.

The room was gloomy, and in contrast to the dry atmosphere outside the door, a dank cold that clung to the skin hung in the air inside. Deeper in the apartment, just like his own, was a bathroom immediately to the right, and on the other side of the short hall, just like his, was a combined living and dining room.

He could make out a light dully reflecting off something inside.

Just then, that light turned and charged toward him. "Wah!" He barely managed to get out of its way; at the same time, a high-pitched noise echoed right by his ear.

A silver meat knife stuck out of the wall beside him.

*Yikes...*

He watched the handle tremble slightly and shuddered, then

turned a bitter gaze inside the apartment; a woman with long hair stood in the doorway to the dining area. As she fixed a hollow glare on him, there was absolutely no sign of life in her face—but never mind that; more importantly, the angle of her neck was strange. It tilted ninety degrees to the right, like a broken doll's.

Knives and forks floated up into the air, as if gravity no longer restrained them in the space around the woman, and hung still, pointing at him.

"Um, hey, I'm not here to see you…," Harvey offered, trying to talk her out of it; but, realizing that he might be at a slight disadvantage, he used his peripheral vision to check escape routes—then he gulped involuntarily. Suddenly, a man was standing so close behind him that he practically had his chin on Harvey's shoulder, directing an unfocused gaze forward.

"Stop it. This man is our guest," he soothed the woman in a monotone voice, then abruptly swiveled his eyes in their sockets, fixing them on Harvey and forming a strangely flat smile. "Pardon her. My wife is a little neurotic," the man said, grinning, a knife sticking out of the left side of his chest.

The "parent-and-child stew," consisting of poultry, eggs, and chickpeas, was the popular dish of Buzz & Suzie's Café, and many of their customers ordered it as soon as they were seated. When Kieli first visited the café, she found herself just copying those around her and asking for the same thing.

Harvey was extremely well-informed, though he didn't look it. (It was rude to say it that way, but apparently to most outsiders, he looked as if he was never really thinking about anything.) He knew more than Kieli about just about everything; when it came to food, though, maybe because he had no interest in it, he lacked common sense at times. When he whispered, "Are chickpeas born from birds?" the woman who had just shown up with their food heard him, and she laughed so hard she slipped and fell, hurting her back.

That was how Kieli met the female owner of this establishment, Suzie.

So, in a way, it was thanks to Harvey that Kieli was able to get a part-time job at this café. However, birds do not birth chickpeas. She smiled whenever she thought of it.

"Hey, take this. Outside."

"Yes, sir."

A goofy grin had appeared on Kieli's face without her knowing it, but when she heard the gruff voice from behind the counter, she stifled it. A stern man's arm reached out from the open kitchen and placed bowls full of hot, milky stew on the counter.

The cook at Buzz & Suzie's Café and Suzie's husband, Buzz was a big, burly, silent man with a thick beard, who looked much more suited to skinning and skewering sand lions in the rocky mountains than specializing in soft meals made with milk. Kieli had been working there for three weeks but still jumped a little when accepting the orders from this giant man with the scary face.

But there was one thing that she and Buzz had in common to talk about. Surprisingly, this man also liked the music, forbidden by the Church, called "rock."

These days, when Kieli arrived in the morning, her first job was to put the radio on a corner of the counter near the kitchen and turn on the up-tempo music found on the guerrilla channels. They couldn't be so bold as to make it the café's background music, so she set it to a very low volume so that only Buzz, in the kitchen, could hear it. Still, some of the regular male customers who came to talk to Buzz over the counter would notice and stop to listen for a while. According to the Corporal, "*All men like rock by nature.*" Kieli didn't really understand, but she supposed it was true.

"Kieli. When you've taken that to its table, can I ask you to do some shopping?" A bright voice reached her from inside the restaurant as she was about to leave the counter, stew in hand.

"Sure, I'll go," she answered, turning. Suzie, who had just come out of the back room, tossed her a folded shopping list and the key to the three-wheeled motorbike. Kieli hurried to balance the bowls of stew in one hand as she caught the bundle with the other.

Suzie was bright, cheerful, and very attentive, but sometimes she did slightly crass things like this, which was how she could occasionally laugh so that hard she fell over. She walked with a cane in one hand to support the hip she'd injured in the incident. In a corner of her mind, Kieli thought, "She must be feeling well today."

Kieli noticed that she had been superimposing her mother onto Suzie just a little. Although it wasn't as if the short, plump Suzie and her slender mother with her clean-cut demeanor looked or acted much alike.

Kieli turned back to the counter one more time and pulled the radio's cord toward her in a rather awkward pose, as she still held the stew. As he turned a frying pan in the kitchen,

Buzz glared her way (but he always looked like that; she didn't *think* he was in a bad mood…probably) but immediately returned his attention to his work. He didn't ask why Kieli always kept the radio somewhere she could see it, but he seemed to understand. Normally, anyone would think it a little strange for this girl to wander into the neighborhood and rent an apartment with a guy who had a fake arm, and Kieli couldn't complain if people kept their distance, but Buzz and Suzie treated her completely normally, as if there were no reason not to.

That's the kind of couple they were, and that's why Kieli liked working at their diner.

She went through the hall, bustling with hungry customers, and out the open glass door onto the squalid, one-lane hill road in front of the restaurant. Two three-wheeled trucks loaded with fossil fuels passed in a line down the street in front of her. As the name, Mine Street, suggested, if she followed the path all the way up to the top of the slope, she would reach the coal mine towering behind the town. Most of the patrons of the diner were miners there.

It had gotten pretty warm, so they had set up some tables on the footpath in front of the café the week before, and miners who had come for an early lunch talked and laughed as they waited for their food. They were in the middle of a sloping path, so the chairs and tables slanted a bit on the uneven ground, but no one seemed to care.

"Thank you very much for waiting," Kieli greeted them, still unused to the phrase, and put the food on the table. No one seemed to care that the bowls slanted, too, as they tasted their stew.

Apparently the residents of this town were rather tolerant of slanting. Not only did the old buildings on the intricate hilly roads crowd together in a jumble, with no sense of organization, but they were also all built at relatively random angles, so if she looked carefully, she could tell that everything slanted a little. Never mind Harvey, but when Kieli got here, her sense of balance was off for the first few days, and she found herself crashing into poles.

Now that she had been here a month, she had gotten completely used to the scenery, and she really felt she was living here. She hadn't felt this way since her grandmother died, even in Easterbury, where she grew up.

Looking up, she could see the light sand-colored sky between the roofs of the uneven line of houses. She took a deep breath, pulling the pleasant spring air into her lungs.

"I hope we can stay in this town forever...," she muttered, half to herself and half to the radio hanging from her hand along with the key to the three-wheeled motorbike.

"...*Unfortunately, Kieli, that's probably not possible,*" she heard a staticky male voice reply through the speaker of the radio over the faint music of stringed instruments.

"I know," Kieli answered, still looking up at the sky, regretting getting carried away in her good mood and blurting out something so irresponsible. She didn't know if Harvey had come here with some goal in mind or if he had just felt like it (she tried asking, but as usual, she didn't get much of an explanation), but either way, he probably had no intention of staying in the same place forever.

It could be said that the life of an Undying is eternal and unchanging, so why did she get the feeling that his way of life was so fleeting?

❧

"Oh, my, what am I doing!? You're a friend of our daughter's, aren't you? You should have said so sooner."

*We're not really "friends."* …

"Please, please, come in and make yourself at home. We don't have much, but…"

*Well, I can see you don't have much.* …

"Now that everyone's here, we have to hurry and get ready for the party!"

*Hey, don't include me. What am I doing here anyway?* As Harvey mocked himself for faithfully responding, in his head, to every sentence, he was half-shoved inside the apartment. He sighed, realizing he'd gotten mixed up with some guys that were going to be a different kind of annoying than he had expected.

The man with the knife in his chest and the woman with the broken neck hurried in and out of the dining area, exchanging shrill conversation.

"We should use those, dear. Would you get out those plates? The ones we got as a wedding gift." "You threw them in a fit of hysteria." "Oh, come now, I would never break such valuable china." "Then maybe I took them to the pawnshop." "That must be it. What am I to do with you? You trade everything for money and use it all for gambling, hee hee hee." "No, but you broke them. You threw them, cabinet and all, remember? Ah-ha-ha-ha." As they talked congenially about such brutal things, their expressions were strangely empty, and their eyes remained unfocused. The scene made Harvey dizzy with its three levels of inconsistency; he looked away, and his eyes met those of a shadow, looking at him from the doorway in the side of the dining room.

That instant, the other person quickly ducked out of sight.

As for the couple in the dining room, they continued their monotonous chitchat as they set the table, but the conversation had completely devolved into a war of insults.

Harvey shrugged and retreated to the wall, then slipped through the door to the bedroom where the shadow had disappeared.

A slender beam of light shone through the small window, casting a spot of faded sand-colored sunlight onto a corner of the room. Under the light was a child's bed. A small person curled up under a comforter of quilted scraps, hiding.

Wordlessly, he stood by the bed and slowly pulled the fork he had been clutching out of the pocket of his work pants. He sensed the shadow under the blanket wince and stiffen. He looked casually down at the fork's tines, giving off a dull light in the sunshine, and the shadow on the bed abruptly jumped up, shouting, "Gyaaa! Murderer!"

Harvey hadn't expected that, and he went speechless for a second, then responded, "No, um, look, wait a minute."

"Help! Don't kill me!"

"Hey, before you start…"

"Nooo! He's gonna kill me!" The shadow refused to listen to what he had to say and kept wailing from the corner of the bed, head in hands. "Help! Stop! Aaaaah!"

"……" Harvey started to get annoyed. "Shut up. Be quiet."

He threw the fork unceremoniously from his hand. It flew through the shadow and stuck into the wall with a *thunk;* at the same time, the screaming stopped.

"You're already long dead anyway."

"...Tch. You're no fun." The shadow pouted and frowned. *You little brat...If you had a body, I'd want to slug it.*

The pajamas were completely plain, but it was a girl wearing them. She was a good talker, but it was hard to tell if her age had reached two digits yet. As for why a child like her would be dead—he didn't care about the details. He hadn't come here to sympathize.

"So? You got something against my roommate?" He finally got to the point, lowering his voice. It seemed he'd had to take quite a useless detour for such a simple matter.

It was this girl who'd dropped something when Kieli passed under her each morning, starting with the paper airplane two days ago, then the marble and the fork. He had left her alone, figuring it was just a little prank, but when it got to a fork, it wasn't a joke anymore.

"Lots," the ghost girl answered, puffing out her chest proudly. "Because she's so healthy and goes out every morning."

"Hmm..."

Just as he started seriously thinking that it might solve things neatly to bring the radio and have him blow her away with a shock wave, now the girl suddenly slumped her shoulders and put on a depressed expression. She directed her downcast gaze at the windowsill and narrowed her eyes at the outside light, as if it was too bright, or, depending on how you looked at her, as if it annoyed her.

"When I was alive, I almost never got to go outside. They said I was born with a blood disease. If I moved just a little, I could get a bruise, and the bleeding wouldn't stop. If I kept taking medicine, I could have gotten a little better, but it was really expensive." She shifted her gaze from the window to the bedroom door. "That's why my parents were always fighting." The girl hung her head in self-derision.

Just then, the shrill sound of shattering glass echoed from the other side of the door.

"It's all your fault. It's your fault we're so poor." "It's not my fault we're poor; it's because the girl was born like that." "It's your fault she was born that way. If only she weren't like that. ..." The discussion between the man and woman was as monotone and rapid-fire as ever; the expression vanished from the girl's face when she heard the exchange.

The couple's conversation suddenly broke off, and an awkward silence hung in the air.

A few seconds later, the woman with the broken neck and the man with the knife in his chest appeared side by side in the bedroom doorway. They plastered friendly smiles on their faces, gauging the girl's mood.

"Um, did you hear what we just said?"

The girl glanced blankly at her father and mother. "No. What was it?" she answered, wearing a fake smile. Maybe her parents didn't notice the subtle movement of their daughter's visage; they looked thoroughly relieved.

"We're almost ready for the party. Come on out."

"You, too, sir. This way, please," they said, and both disappeared again into the dining room.

He was silent for some reason as he watched them go, then looked back at the bed, where the girl was conscientiously pulling a cardigan over her pajamas, despite just being a ghost.

"It's my birthday party. If I was alive, I'd be ten. But I died the day before my birthday, so I'll be nine forever. Wanna know why I died?"

"Not really."

"You're no fun. And here I was thinking I might stop bugging that girl if you would give me someone to talk to."

"...I'm going home," Harvey said as he spun around and started to walk toward the door. Having her tread on his weakness and use it as a bargaining chip like that *really* got on his nerves—no, maybe he was mad at himself that it actually was a weakness, and he felt like he might accept her terms because of it, but never mind that. If she really wasn't going to stop, then he just had to get serious and have the Corporal blast her.

"Come on, wait! Aren't you coming to my birthday party?"

"Why should I have to go to a party for someone who's got nothing to do with me?" he answered without even turning around.

"Nothing to do with you? You're mean, mister!" the girl's voice chased after him, a little dramatically. "I mean, we're kind of the same, aren't we? Mister Undying."

He stopped. So she had realized—it wouldn't really cause him any problems for a ghost to know, but he naturally put up his guard as he turned around.

The girl sat on the edge of the bed in her dimly lit bedroom, swinging her bare feet back and forth.

"I know all about Undyings. You're alive, but you're not. No matter how much everything changes around you, you're the only thing that doesn't change, and time leaves you behind—just like me; I'll always be nine years old. No matter how many times my birthday comes and we celebrate it, I'll never be ten years old. See? We're the same, right?"

"I…" he started automatically, but even he didn't know how he'd meant to finish that sentence. The girl smiled with an expression that seemed innocent at first, but seemed to hint at something—a kind of look unsuited to someone her age.

"You're coming to my party, right?"

Kieli fastened four large cans of milk and a paper bag full of onions to the three-wheeled bike's rack, then started up the sloping Mine Street to Buzz & Suzie's Café.

In this town made entirely of hills, the three-wheeled motorbike was commonly used as a mode of transportation. There was no clutch, and anyone could control the accelerator and brakes with just the handles, so it was pretty simple. After learning from Suzie and practicing for a day, even Kieli could more or less drive one.

The luggage rack was extremely big, but its inside was mostly occupied by the gas tank with its inefficient fossil fuel. Exhaust spouted out of the clumsy muffler sticking out the back, creating an immense nuisance to the neighborhood, as she flew by the pedestrians. Nevertheless, from what she could see, it didn't really bother anyone, and laundry still hung calmly out to dry in the house windows.

The exhaust, along with the slanting, must have been an everyday thing for this town.

Even though the roads were paved, they were cracked and bumpy due to the high traffic of trucks carrying fuel, and she didn't go very fast. The streets on either side of her passed by at a peaceful pace along with the spring wind that felt nice on her skin.

*"It's okay to be a little extra cheerful today. It is your birthday."*

"Yeah…" Kieli agreed, a little inarticulately, with the voice from the radio hanging around her neck. "But it's just a day my grandmother decided on; it's not my actual birthday."

A day on the border between spring and winter—the last day of winter before spring term started—had become Kieli's birthday. Apparently, her grandmother picked the last day of the school year for the simple reason that Kieli was small, so she called it her birthday, but it meant nothing more than, "I might be around fifteen years old today."

"I should have asked my mom when my birthday is…." She spoke what was on her mind, and immediately regretted it.

Her mother slept at the final destination of the Sand Ocean—Kieli thought she had gotten over it, but as it really was painful to remember, she did her utmost not to think about it.

Maybe Harvey was being considerate, or maybe he just didn't care, but anyway, he hadn't mentioned it since then. It seemed as though the man named Jude who was with her mother (she still didn't really know if he was her father or not) was someone Harvey knew a long time ago, and Harvey seemed unusually insistent—for him—on learning about him. At a certain point, though, he suddenly stopped bringing it up, as if it no longer mattered to him.

When she thought about it, she got the feeling that that certain point happened about when they arrived in this town.

From South-hairo port, the western entrance to the southeast continent, the train tracks went due east and ran into the line of mountains that divided the huge South-hairo parish between east and west. This town stood as if someone had cut out a part of that line and glued it back on at an angle. The reason it had so many sloping roads was its location.

Yellowish gray smoke rose from the cluster of exhaust pipes at the very top of the slopes, at the peak of the fault, painting the sandy clouds in the sky an even thicker color. Some dregs of the fossilized resources that had dried up during the War still remained inside the mountains, and the mine tunnel had been dug in order to find them. Apparently there were a few other mining towns like this left in South-hairo, but of them, this one was especially big and bustling.

They'd arrived at port about two months ago. They had continued their fairly freewheeling—or at least it seemed freewheeling to Kieli—train travel, stopping at stations along the way, but for some reason, apparently Harvey felt like stopping and settling down in this city.

"*All he said was, 'We're gonna be living here for a while.' Damn, what is he thinking?*"

"He might not be thinking of anything, you know."

"*No, but hey, he looks as if he's just lying around, not doing anything, and then sometimes he'll actually look at the time and go out. It's downright fishy, if you ask me.*"

"There's your weird detective spirit getting fired up again...," Kieli muttered in exasperation, although she had been wondering the same thing. Once or twice a week, he would wander out at night and not come back until morning. It was suspicious that the one time she asked him where he was going, all he said was "Cards." It was true that there were days when he went to the gambling house in the business district, but to Harvey, gambling seemed to be something to pay for necessary expenses, not something he actually enjoyed, so it was difficult to think that he'd get so caught up in it that he'd be gone all night long.

He suddenly said they were going to live here for a while, just went and rented an apartment, and for all that he didn't seem to really be doing anything—he just stayed in the apartment every day except when he would wander off somewhere. Even when Kieli, bored with so much free time, used Suzie's injury as an opportunity to say she wanted to help at the diner, the only reaction he gave was, "Sure, why not? Go ahead."

She hadn't thought about it much before because when they were traveling they'd never stayed in one place for very long, but now that they had settled down in town like this, she thought that Harvey wasn't really suited to living in society. Maybe it was because he was so used to traveling alone, but he basically did whatever he pleased. He lived life at random hours, couldn't fit in with other people, thought it was a pain to deal with others....

Thinking about these things, she actually felt a bit superior, though her feelings weren't really directed at anyone. Harvey was the way he was, but at least he allowed Kieli to enter his field of vision; and as of yet, he hadn't abandoned her, choosing instead to stay with her.

*"What are you smiling about?"*

"Nothing." She dodged the dubious question from under her chin, and while she was at it, she increased her sluggish pace slightly. The sound of the fossil fuel engine may have enveloped their conversation, but if anyone passing by saw her grinning and talking to herself, that person would think she was weird.

*"What's with you, smiling all weird like that?"*

"It's nothing. I'm just looking forward to tonight."

*"You can't expect anything thoughtful from him, you know."*

"I'm not. It would be creepy if he did do anything thoughtful for me." Kieli felt that if something like that happened, she would worry about Harvey's ulterior motive. Like maybe he would be gone when she woke up the next morning.

Fears like that would sometimes suddenly occur to her before she fell asleep. When she would crawl out of bed and peer into the dining room, Harvey would be sitting on the sofa, smoking a cigarette and gazing out the window into the night without really looking at anything. That made Kieli feel better, and she would sneak back into bed.

*"Have him buy you something. He can make as much money as he wants when he puts his mind to it."*

"But what do I want...?"

She thought about it for a bit, then answered, "Nothing especially." Well, it wasn't as if there was absolutely nothing. It was helpful to have clothes and daily necessities, and the radio's cord was getting pretty beat up. She could pay for those things with her own wages, though, so she didn't see a need to specifically ask for them.

Now, more than anything, it was enough just to have someone to spend her birthday with. The last time she remembered anyone celebrating with her was her eighth birthday, just before her grandmother died. All her birthdays after that were nothing but melancholy days of packing her things so she could change rooms in the boarding house, thinking things like, "So spring term starts tomorrow. It's hard having to make friends with a new roommate and new classmates."

*Oh, I remember.* But last year, she had had a birthday party for the first time in a while. It wasn't for her, though; it was for her roommate.

Becca's birthday, according to the ghost herself, was in the middle of summer, so they'd taken advantage of everyone being gone for the summer holidays to sneak into the school's chapel and have fun playing with the organ together.

When they'd sunk to the floor, tired from all the merry-making, Becca had smiled and said slowly, "But I won't get older anymore."

*...If Becca did grow up, I think she would be so pretty.* A woman with golden hair down to her hips, fluttering in the wind as she walked briskly down the street—Kieli could imagine it so clearly it was as if Becca was actually in front of her. Men wouldn't be able to help stopping and turning when she passed by.

*"Kieli, watch out!"*

"Eh?"

She automatically grabbed the brakes in response to the radio's shout, and at the same time, the grown-up Becca standing in front of her turned in her direction.

There was a dull thud at the front wheel.

*...I hit her.*

It took her a few seconds to realize.

The paper bag came loose from the luggage rack, and onions tumbled down the sloping road. As she listened to the strangely peaceful rolling sound in a corner of her consciousness, she

gazed dumbly at the woman on the ground a few meters ahead of her. Passersby gathered noisily around them.

"...*Kieli. Hey*," the radio whispered, in a similarly dumbfounded but urgent voice, and the girl came back to her senses.

"A-are you all right!?"

Kieli practically flung the bike aside as she jumped off and ran to the woman she'd struck. The pedestrian picked herself up, shaking her head. *Oh good, she's alive!* There was no doubt she had done something terrible, but still, Kieli was somewhat relieved. "Are you injured? Do you hurt anywhere? I'm sorry! I wasn't paying attention. I thought you were an illusion. I was thinking about my friend, and, um! I'm really sorry!" She rattled off things that didn't make sense even to her as she peered into the face of the woman sitting on the asphalt.

That instant, Kieli cut herself off, and her eyes widened.

*Becca!*

The woman really looked exactly like the adult version of Becca that Kieli had just imagined. Her long blond hair with a slight wave to it, her clear blue eyes...

"Oh, I'm fine. I just fell trying to dodge." Even her bright, carefree smile and her manner of speech when she answered were exactly like Becca.

Surprise and relief struck Kieli speechless as she continued to gape, and the woman blinked and said, "Hey, are *you* okay?" while waving a hand in front of Kieli's face.

"Yes! Um, I was thinking how pretty you are...," she blurted. When she realized how absurd she sounded, Kieli turned bright red and jumped back.

"Thank you," the woman said smoothly, smiling, without anything like modesty. Then she waved her hand again, this time to shoo away the gathering onlookers—"Okay, there was no accident here. Go on, get out of here"—and it felt good to hear her unaffected, sociable tone.

A few passersby (all of them male) had come over to lend a hand, but they went off, seeming somehow disappointed.

The woman stood up, brushing the dust off her clothes, so Kieli stood up with her. She breathed a sigh of relief to see that her victim wasn't really hurt, then hung her head again.

"I really am sorry."

"Oh, don't worry about it. It's partly my fault for jumping out in front of you. Some weirdo just wouldn't leave me alone." She scanned her surroundings, looking thoroughly disgusted, and after a bit, she relaxed and softened her expression. "It looks like he disappeared in the commotion. You actually helped me out."

*She's a nice person.* Kieli felt better. The more she looked at the beautiful woman, the more the woman looked identical to Becca. She appeared to be about Harvey's age, or maybe a little older. In a corner of her mind, Kieli wondered if she herself would be a good match for Harvey when she got to that age, but she had a hunch that train of thought wouldn't lead anywhere pleasant, so she stopped.

Instead, she remembered the onions.

"Aahh!"

She looked back at the bike, but every single onion had fallen out of the bag on the rack and had long since vanished from sight at the bottom of the slope. She panicked and ran back, turning her head halfway to say, "I work at Buzz & Suzie's Café at the top of the hill; please come by if you like. I'll treat you, as an apology!"

Kieli didn't wait for an answer as she straddled the driver's seat and started the engine. After a pause, black smoke spouted out of the muffler, along with the sound of a cheap motor. As she twisted the accelerator in an effort to get the bike to face downward, she suddenly heard the radio's voice. "*Hey, wait a second. Look. In front.*" Easy for him to say, but as Kieli didn't know where to look, her gaze wandered for a while before her eyes stopped on the front wheel's fender.

The metal plate was spectacularly dented.

Now that she thought about it, the woman said she just fell, but Kieli was sure she had felt an impact.

"Um…!"

By the time she turned around, the woman had disappeared into the crowd of people coming and going along the street.

"Mama and Papa went though a lot of trouble because I was born like this. Papa started gambling to earn money for my medicine, but he went into debt instead, and Mama had a terrible time taking care of me because I kept crying about how much it hurt every single night, and she went crazy. They said I wouldn't live to be ten years old, but my tenth birthday was coming up and I was still alive. Mama and Papa were so exhausted because I lived much longer than they'd thought, and we were out of money, so the day before my birthday, they couldn't take it anymore and our family ended in a murder-suicide." The girl related the story indifferently as she used her fork to stab at the chocolate cake on her plate.

"Then, the next thing I knew, we were having a birthday party. We have a party every day. Every single day, and nothing I do can stop it."

The utensils were real, but the cake was nothing more than an illusion painted before her. Every time the girl stabbed her cake, the fork would hit the plate with a high-pitched clank. To a normal person, it would probably look as though the fork was floating on its own and hitting a barren plate.

That would be a chilling scene in itself, but Harvey thought he could safely say the scene he was witnessing was even more bizarre.

Chipped plates and rusted cutlery crammed the dining table, and countless elegant foods, out of balance with the humble tableware, sat on top of them. But the assortment was somehow mismatched or, to put it bluntly, lacking in good taste. (Not that he really had any place judging, when it came to food.) A giant guinea fowl cooked whole; a frighteningly sweet-looking three-layer chocolate cake (*Three layers! who's gonna eat that?*); mutton sausage; and a combination platter of whole fruits—they'd just indiscriminately conjured up whatever first came to mind when you thought of a "feast."

The mother with the broken neck gazed on them with a proud but somehow vacant, cheap smile and encouraged the girl to eat one thing after another. The father with the knife in his chest grinned and offered Harvey a plate. "Now, now. Don't be shy; you have some, too. This is the first time we've had a guest for our daughter's birthday."

Harvey rested his chin in his hand with his elbow on the

table, directing his eyes nowhere in particular, and answered only, "Thanks." He ignored the food (or rather, the chipped plate with nothing on it).

He'd already asked himself several times today, but from the depths his heart, he thought, *What am I doing?*

Sure, he might not be able to go home until he got the girl to stop harassing Kieli, but even he thought it was incredibly stupid to get carried away by events enough to stick around.

He looked over at the birthday girl sitting in the so-called "birthday seat" diagonally across from him. She wasn't bringing the food to her mouth either, but rather thrusting her fork into it and yanking it out in a way that almost looked like she was trying to destroy it.

"I'm tired of this. Every day the same birthday, every day the same feast. And I never once said I wanted to eat any of this stuff," she spat in a low voice.

Harvey averted his eyes from her face without a word and cast a sideways glance at her parents, who were quarreling at the center of the table as they cut up the roasted bird.

He looked back at the girl and opened his mouth. "What *do* you want to do?"

"Eh?" The girl stopped stabbing with her fork, a blank expression on her face.

"Your parents are just doing their best to make you happy, aren't they?"

"Their 'best' is just empty effort. I mean, this stuff doesn't make me happy at—"

"So I'm asking what you *do* want to do," said Harvey, his tone growing harsh as annoyance started to set in. "You're stuck in this loop because you have some lingering regret, right? There's something else, isn't there? Something you want to do that's not a party."

"...There is!" the girl said energetically, then, "But—" She cut herself off and hung her head. In the silence, the parents' voices, in their ever-monotonous chatter, reached his ears, along with a surreal feeling, like background music from behind a screen.

After a little while, the girl continued haltingly. "But I know they'll say I can't, so it's pointless to even ask."

"I'm *telling* you, just say what you want. You won't know until you ask." *Argh, this is irritating.* That thought probably contained some annoyance at himself for saying stuff like this to a complete stranger. This was getting to be a pain, so Harvey lumped all the irritation together and directed it at her parents. "Hey, listen to her. Stop just bickering back and forth!"

The parents, who had been arguing about whether to start cutting the guinea fowl from its head or its tail (*Who the hell cares?*), stopped abruptly, and the meat knife slipped out of their hands, its blade sticking into the table with a *thunk*.

They concentrated their stares at the girl, who faltered and winced a little. She threw a sideways glance at Harvey, as if pleading for help. "Go on, say it," he urged with a sigh.

The girl turned her eyes up at her parents, looking from one to the other, then, with a meek expression, opened her mouth. "...Um, hey. You promised on my ninth birthday, remember? If I lived to be ten, you would take me outside town. I want to try going to the top of the hill. At the very, very top you can see a spaceship on the other side, right? I want to see the spaceship."

She got that far and clammed up. Timidly, but with the faintest hope in her eyes, she checked her parents' reactions.

Her parents exchanged a troubled look.

"But you couldn't," her father said, shaking his head regretfully. "You'd have to climb a lot of hills and stairs. You can't be outside for that long, you know."

Her mother nodded in agreement, "He's right. What if you start hurting before we get there? What if you get a scrape and can't stop bleeding?"

"Never mind!" The girl's abrupt shout interrupted her parents. "See? I told you they'd say no. They just promised me that to get me to be quiet. I mean, look, there was no way I could have lived to be ten," she said in a joking tone and shrugged at Harvey. But she suddenly averted her eyes and hung her head, biting her lip as if she was holding something in. Her father started to open his mouth again but ended up just swallowing his words awkwardly, and a heavy silence enveloped the dining room.

After a few seconds, Harvey finally interjected, "...Hey." His timing was thrown off by the oppressive atmosphere, but this was getting to be too much. The girl and her parents glanced up, still looking depressed. "Well, er..." He got the feeling that having the whole ghost family look at him with those dejected faces might get him cursed, and faltering a little, he asked the girl, "You wanna go now?"

"...Huh?"

The girl just blinked with a blank expression, so her father raised his voice angrily instead. "Please don't say those irresponsible things!" Following suit, her mother spoke, in almost a scream, "You're terrible! You only say that because you don't know! You don't know how pitiful this girl is, how painful her attacks are!"

He noticed the plates on the table starting to shake in concert with the mother's outburst. Then, in defiance of the laws of physics, they floated upward. Knives and forks rotated in the air and then pointed his way, taking aim.

"Wait a—Listen! Maybe when she was alive, but she's already—" he added in a panic as he got up from his chair, but he stumbled on its legs, and while he was distracted, a fork flew at him like an arrow. It sliced a few millimeters of skin off his cheek and pierced the wall behind him.

He shuddered and shouted, "She's already dead! She won't have any attacks!"

"Mama, stop!" The girl's voice overlapped his, and a knife stopped abruptly, right at the tip of his nose.

Harvey had a staring match with the point of the knife floating in front of him and gulped unconsciously—that instant, as if its strings had been cut, the knife dropped straight down, and a dry clatter echoed from the floor.

Harvey let out a deep breath he didn't know he had been holding.

"You're just letting the way things were when you were alive hold you back. She really won't have any more attacks—she doesn't have a body. If she wants to go outside, she could just pass through the wall and go," he said in a somewhat softer tone than usual, looking toward the girl. She had frozen in a half-standing position, about to cry.

Then he shifted his focus to the girl's parents. "Ah…," the two said dumbly as they stood gaping side by side on the other side of the table, then both clapped their hands together, looking as if they finally understood.

"Now that you mention it, you're right."

"Now that he mentions it, he's right."

Harvey was getting a headache.

"I can go outside...?" the girl asked nervously. "But I've hardly been outside at all since I was little, because I get attacks right away...."

"I'm telling you, you won't have an attack." *You still won't believe me?* Harvey sighed in exasperation. "The other side of the top of the slope, right?"

*What am I doing?* He inwardly recited the line that he had been muttering all day and vowed to himself that no matter what happened in the future, no matter how long he lived, he would never, ever, under any circumstances, help another stranger this much again.

"I'll take you there. Come on," he said, offering his hand to the girl.

Kieli's work for the day at Buzz & Suzie's Café ended with taking the chairs from the outside tables inside and hanging the CLOSED sign on the door. She carried the last chair to a corner of the hall and was about to go flip the sign when Suzie suggested she eat dinner before she went.

Kieli thanked her but shook her head. "You see, I have plans today. It's my birthday."

After a brief pause, Suzie suddenly got angry. "Your birthday? Today? Why didn't you tell us sooner? Just what kind of people do you think we are?!" Suzie ranted as Kieli stood in dumbfounded bewilderment; then Buzz just said, "Wait there," shutting himself up in the kitchen. After thirty minutes, he came back out with a freshly baked pound cake.

Still in shock, Kieli let them press the package with the pound cake into her hands and let Suzie rant at her some more about how that skinny boy (*boy?*) she lived with probably wasn't eating properly, and she should bring him here to eat sometime. At length, they finally released her, and she put the diner behind her.

"That was a surprise.... I didn't think she'd get mad at me for saying it's my birthday."

As she trudged up the slope that led to their apartment, carrying her bag, the radio, and the pound cake, Kieli was still stunned.

*"They thought you were treating them like strangers."*

"But they *are* strangers...." After she answered, for some reason her own words struck at her heart. But at this point in her life, the only people Kieli could say were not strangers to her were Harvey and the Corporal.

*"Sussy doesn't think so."*

"Suzie," she corrected him, as Harvey had done so many times. When Kieli announced that she was thinking of working at Buzz & Suzie's Café, the first thing Harvey'd said was, "Sure, why not?" but the Corporal's immediate reaction was that it was too hard to say with all the Zs.

*"You're not as bad as Herbie, but you draw too many boundaries between yourself and others."*

"Harvey." As she corrected him again, Kieli wondered if he was right.

One person's footsteps and two voices resounded quietly in the empty night street, like static in the air.

The day's work at the mine ended as the sun went down, and the miners went home, making people scarce relatively early on Mine Street. Almost all the shops lining both sides of the avenue had closed, and the yellow glow spilling out of windows from upper floors and the dull light of streetlamps made spots here and there on the now blue-gray asphalt. After being so noisy and overflowing with activity during the day, the street seemed even emptier than it actually was after the sun set.

Although it was the beginning of spring, the night wind was still chilly, and Kieli hunched her shoulders a little, clutching the paper bag in her hands to her chest. She felt the warmth of fresh pound cake and smelled its faint fragrance.

"Come to think of it, she didn't come to the diner after all," Kieli murmured, remembering the face of the woman she had crashed into that afternoon—the beautiful blond woman who looked like Becca.

"I wonder if she's really okay. I hope she's not passed out somewhere right now...."

*"She said herself she was fine, so she's probably fine."*

"But the bike was dented. What did I hit?"

*"Forget it. She's fine."*

"Corporal?" She looked down at the radio, wondering about his strangely blunt tone.

After a moment of silence, the radio said, *"Oh, don't worry about it. There's just something about her."*

Now that her companion was speaking normally, Kieli wondered even more. She furrowed her brow, but he forced the conversation to a close, saying, *"No, I'll tell you about it later. I have to check something with Herbie."*

"Hmm...," Kieli murmured, sounding somewhat dissatisfied, and took her eyes off the radio. So there were things the

Corporal could talk to Harvey about but not to her. There wasn't much reason for it, but she was a little disappointed.

The apartment came into view at the top of the hill. The reddish gray, five-story building stood tightly squished between similar, but slightly leaning, buildings on either side and in front of it.

She looked casually up at a window on the third floor and stopped for a second.

"Huh…?"

The light wasn't on. The glass inside the window frame had sunken into pitch darkness.

Kieli started walking again, her pace quickening in the first two or three steps, and by the time she turned around the side of the building, she was jogging; she ran up the outside stairway to the third floor in one bound, the radio bouncing as she went. She carefully hid the unevenness of her breath as she stood in front of the door, shifted the pound cake to her side, and put her hand on the knob.

It was unlocked, and her hopes rose a little, but when she opened the door halfway and peeked inside, it was still completely dark, and she sensed no sign of anyone inside.

"*Where the hell did he go without locking the door? How can he be so careless?*" the radio cursed. Kieli didn't say a word as she slowly pushed the door closed behind her. She made her way into the dining room without turning on the lights.

Faint illumination from the streetlamps shone in from under the window, casting a bluish glow above the sofa. The deserted sofa seemed to float, the only thing lit up in the gloom, and looked strangely forlorn.

"But he promised…." The murmur escaped her lips haltingly, before she was aware of it.

"*Kieli*…" The radio's anxious voice came to her. "*He'll be right back, I'm sure. He just went somewhere nearby, that's all.*"

"Oh, it's okay. It's not like we were gonna do anything special, and Harvey probably won't eat any cake anyway, so let's just eat it without him," she said quickly, then, "Oh, you won't be eating it, either, will you, Corporal…." She trailed off and closed her mouth.

She meaninglessly surveyed the dining room one more time, as if she expected to find something, then left the package of cake on the dining room table. It made a more violent sound than she expected.

*Damn it, this is farther than I thought.*

But Harvey didn't realize that until, well, after they had gotten there. He seemed to remember that the one time he went there before it took only about thirty minutes, but even he realized that his sense of time was pretty arbitrary. If someone were to ask him if it really did take thirty minutes, he wouldn't have confidence that he was right. He didn't even remember how many years ago it had been.

After climbing to the top of Mine Street, passing beside the mining building, taking a narrow path even higher up, then climbing even farther up a stairway that crawled zigzagging along the stone wall towering behind the city, they reached the peak of the fault, the very top of the slope. By the time they got there, naturally, the sun had set. With the faint city lights that reached them from far below, back down the way they had come, Harvey could just make out the bare rock beneath his feet.

The dry wind from the wilderness would sometimes gust by, ruffling his hair. Unlike the air he felt in town, with its sense of life, this air had the scent of desolate earth. It wasn't as if he had any good memories of such places, but if he had to choose, he was more familiar with this wind, and it felt more comfortable to him.

"It's pitch-black."

The girl in pajamas stood on tiptoe next to him and squinted into the distance. Harvey lit a cigarette and feigned ignorance.

"'Cause it's night...."

"I can't see a thing. And we came all this way! That's no fun." The girl frowned.

Wondering why this girl who couldn't just tell her parents what she wanted had no reservations about shooting off complaints to him, Harvey sighed and indicated far into the dark night with the fingers that held his cigarette.

"You can kind of make out a black shadow sticking out over there, right? That's the ruins of the spaceship."

"Mmm?"

The girl just tilted her head and made a vague response, so he felt a little discouraged inside. *She can't see it?* He re-created the scene in his mind from when he'd gazed on it before, though he didn't remember how long ago it had been.

Under the sky, pierced by the dull sunlight between the sand-colored clouds, the bare, rocky wilderness formed a gentle downward slope that continued far beyond his vision, to the distant horizon and its gaseous haze. Shifting his gaze a little to the right, he could see, in the center of the wilderness, a circular area, the one place of a very slightly different color, where something stuck out of the ground at an angle.

That thing, which looked like a rusty bayonet piercing the earth, was actually an enormous structure—the last interstellar spacecraft, said to have crashed here hundreds of years ago.

It wasn't a very good description, but he explained it to her. The girl didn't seem to get it after all, and adopted a questioning look.

"Why did the spaceship crash?"

"I don't know. But after that last ship crashed there, prisoner escort ships stopped coming to this planet. They say that there was a revolution or something on the mother planet at the same time, but those are just old rumors—they probably have nothing to do with this planet anymore."

"Prisoner escort ships?" The girl responded with another question, confusion in her voice. *Oh, right, this isn't really common knowledge.* Harvey mulled for a bit over how to explain.

"This world was originally an exile planet. A place where they banished prisoners for eternity. They didn't think there was anything on this barren wasteland, but then they found fossilized resources and started using prisoners to mine here. That was when the pioneering age started, and the Church's ship came at the end of that age. They said it was for some noble cause like saving the sinners, but they only came here to get the resources, and that's why you're—" *Why you're probably right that there's no God,* he started to say, then caught his mistake and cut himself off. Without realizing, he had started thinking he was explaining this to Kieli.

The girl looked straight ahead into the darkness. She had said she couldn't see anything, but she gazed forward as if she had found what she was looking for. Apparently she was only half listening to him.

"I think I might be able to see the spaceship," she muttered almost to herself, still directing her eyes forward. "Lots of people are coming out of a big ship and walking this way in a long line, and they're digging a tunnel and building a town and starting to live here." *The ship crashed, so they were probably all dead; I don't think the people living here are from that ship,* Harvey opened his mouth to interject, but gave up. The girl probably was really seeing that right now.

"And the town is getting bigger and bigger, and they're making streets and building houses, and Papa and Mama are being born, and I'm being born." The girl jumped up and turned around.

Harvey blinked, then turned around himself to see an unbroken view of the city lights spreading out below the path they had climbed.

One after another, streetlights rose out of the darkness, indicating Mine Street as it gently wended its way downward, and the warm glow from the windows of houses dotted the scene, scattering grains of light. The cluster of lights twinkling close together at the very bottom was probably the business district downtown.

"This is the first time I've looked at the city from above like this. It's so pretty...."

"You think so?" Harvey answered after a moment. He didn't quite feel strongly enough to sympathize with the girl's murmur of admiration. You could find this scenery in any city, and he thought that if you wanted a nightscape, Westerbury's flock of neon was much more spectacular.

But the girl was completely entranced, and she looked wordlessly down at the city lights for a while.

"Do you like this city, mister?" she asked him without warning. The Undying had never thought about the question she suddenly threw at him, and it took him a minute to respond.

"I don't really like it. But I don't hate it."

"Then start liking it now. I just started liking it now, too."

"That doesn't make sense," he retorted, scowling with his cigarette in his mouth.

But the girl didn't even bother continuing the topic, declaring, "I'm satisfied. Let's go back!" She started running full-speed toward the city lights. She hopped quickly down the paved steps that bent back and forth along the stone wall.

"Hey, hey…!" Harvey tried to stop her, but in the end, he lost all will to say anything and let out a tired, smoky sigh, then started down the steps trailing behind the girl.

As she jumped energetically down the stairs, the ghost turned halfway back toward him and smiled. "You're a nice guy, mister!"

"Gee, thanks," he responded halfheartedly, still walking. Harvey himself was shocked at just how stupidly nice he was being.

"Start liking this city, 'kay?"

The girl repeated her line from before and faced forward again. "Because I finally just started to like it, but I won't be able to like it anymore…." Her back, clad in white pajamas and a cardigan, faded into the air with each step she descended.

The scene beyond her, the faint city lights that floated in the dark night, shone through her.

"So I really hope you'll like it for me."

Her clear, bright voice lingered in his ears as she took a small hop down one more step... and then the girl disappeared in midair, never reaching the next one.

Harvey got back to the apartment building well after midnight. When he visited the apartment on the fifth floor, the girl's parents had already vanished, and only their white dishes remained on the table, as if the family had been eating dinner mere moments before. But the porcelain plates were cracked with layers of dust on top of them, and the tarnished silver cutlery had long since lost its usefulness.

The next-door neighbor would no longer have to fear poltergeists (or the landlord), and there would no longer be any forks falling from the window.

Harvey stood in the doorway for a while, gazing at the desolate space, then left the apartment.

He went back to the third floor, his faint footsteps echoing on the outside stairs. He opened the second door down the hall, the plain door to his own home (although he had forgotten what "my own home" felt like sometime long, long ago, so it didn't quite feel real to him). Late as it was, the inside of the room was silent in slumber. He closed the door softly, so as not to make a sound, and went inside.

He stopped unthinkingly in the door to the dining room

and was about to peer into the bedroom beside it, when he heard a "*Hey…*"

He heard a low, very slightly staticky voice. Its tone was strangled, as if it had crawled up from the depths of the earth, and he gulped and froze in spite of himself, then turned slowly toward the dining room.

A dull, bluish light shone from the window, dimly outlining the sofa underneath it. An old, beat-up little radio sat in its center—leaning a little, as if it had been carelessly abandoned there.

"…What?" Harvey answered, bracing himself somewhat, in a voice quiet enough not to be heard in the bedroom.

"*Just what is your memory made out of? So you never forget stuff that happened eighty years ago, but you have no problem forgetting something that happened just this morning? Why don't you open up that rusty head of yours and wash your brains out? It won't kill ya.*"

Did he have to go that far? "I didn't forget. I feel bad," he retorted, understandably irked.

"*Damn it, does somebody who feels bad…,*" the radio started to yell, but then fell silent, with a short burst of static. After a pause, a quieter voice came from the speaker.

"*Oh, never mind. That's just how you are. I'm so disgusted, I don't wanna say anything anymore.*"

"What? Say it."

"*…Think more about how Kieli feels. That's all,*" the radio spat, and then stopped talking altogether. Usually whenever the Corporal was unhappy about something, he would rant about it until he was done, and Harvey felt as if the radio had actually blown him off.

He glared sulkily at the radio, wondering if he deserved that much wrath, but for some reason he started feeling awkward and looked away, peering again into the bedroom.

Semidarkness enveloped the small room. There was a single pipe bed under the window, and in the faint night light, he could make out a small figure burrowed under the blanket. There was no quilted comforter, but for a second in his mind this bed overlapped with that of the girl from the fifth floor.

She seemed to be sleeping facing the wall, so he walked up and leaned over to look at her. Kieli stirred and rolled onto her stomach.

"What, you were just pretending?"

"...I was asleep. The Corporal's yelling woke me up," she muttered into her pillow, muffling her voice, but after that, she went abruptly silent again. He noticed her slender fists, clutching the blanket so tightly that they were white, and finally sincerely regretted what he had done.

"Uh, um, hey. Something suddenly came up, and I went out for a bit," he began but realized it sounded like a mere excuse and gave up partway through the explanation. He looked upward, in some arbitrary direction, and thought for a few seconds that seemed more like an hour to him before finally coming up with "I'm sorry. I was wrong." He said it with a sigh and hung his head a little while he was at it.

Kieli raised her head slightly, for about one second. "...Whatever, I'm not mad," she replied curtly, and buried her face again. Clearly, she *was* mad.

"...Um, hey. Argh, how can I get you to cheer up?" His speech pattern went a little strange in his utter bewilderment, and he made a face that was sour even for him.

"Cake," Kieli murmured.

"Huh?" Caught off guard, Harvey reflexively answered with a question.

Kieli pulled her cheeks away from the pillow and glared sideways up at him, then, with a scowl, repeated, "Cake."

*What am I doing?*

That must have been the millionth time Harvey had wondered that today. Apparently that was just the kind of day it was, and he sighed in resignation as he gazed at the plate of pound cake that had been handed to him. Why should he have to eat cake he didn't even really want in the middle of the night like this?

He threw a sidelong glance at the girl sitting next to him on the sofa, and for someone who had been so pouty before, she was awfully cheery as she held a fork in one hand and cut up the cake on the small plate in her lap. She brought a small piece to her mouth and tasted it with a complicated expression on her face, then grinned happily from ear to ear. *She may have turned fifteen, but she's definitely no more mature in any way,* he found himself thinking with a strange sense of relief.

"*Like it?*" the radio asked, sitting between them in the middle of the sofa (he had been left there since he got home).

"I wish you could have some, too, Corporal."

"*It's times like this I wish I had possessed a living thing.*"

"Like what?"

"*Like...hmm. A dog or something.*"

"A dog corporal?" Kieli's question sparked Harvey's imagination, and he almost laughed at the image of a dog that came to mind.

"*What?*"

"Nothing." He erased the look from his face and turned away from the radio's displeased voice.

The black windowpane dimly reflected Harvey's profile and the scene in the dining room. As he casually watched the glass, he poked at his plate with the fork in his right hand (he wasn't really right- or left-handed, but fairly ambidextrous; but recently, his prosthetic arm was performing better than his original right arm, so he had sort of become right-handed), and tossed a piece of cake into his mouth. It wasn't as sweet as he expected. He wasn't qualified to say one way or another about how anything tasted, but this might be pretty good.

With the fork in his mouth in place of a cigarette, he sat on the sofa, resting his elbow on the back with his chin in his hand, and dropped his attention past the scene of the room reflected on the window glass, through to the streets below.

A cramped, sloping road stretched to the right and left, with old, iron-framed buildings on either side. There was no movement aside from the weak flicker of streetlamps here and there, and there was a complete sense of quiet slumber. When the miners began work the next morning, though, it would be the start of another bustling day.

Harvey turned his mind to the conversation going on beside him, where Kieli was speaking modestly about how famous a cook the owner of Buzz & Suzie's Café was, and the radio was complaining about how hard it was to pronounce "Buzz & Suzie's Café." The two sides of the conversation didn't quite mesh.

"Kieli, do you like this city?" Harvey articulated the question that suddenly came to mind as he stared out the window.

The conversation broke off, and he sensed Kieli turning to look at him. By that time, he regretted asking such a peculiar question and was about to say "Never mind" when she answered.

It was a short, honest reply. "Yeah. I like it pretty well."

Still resting his chin on his hand, Harvey glanced sideways at her. Kieli contemplated the cake on her lap with a bashful smile and continued. "I like the people here well enough, and I like Buzz and Suzie well enough, and I like working at Buzz & Suzie's Café well enough."

"*I'm telling you, it's hard to say!*" the radio interjected selfishly, bringing the topic back.

Harvey just sighed and didn't join the debate, looking back outside the window.

He paid no heed to the voices of the girl and the radio that reached his ears as he looked down at the streets again. He wondered if he might feel something, but in all honesty, he didn't personally feel any preference. He didn't really have any interest in the people who lived here, and he just didn't care one way or another.

...But he also thought that if Kieli and that girl said so, maybe he could try a little.

"Ah...," he uttered unintentionally. After a pause, he adjusted the fork in his mouth, smiling wryly.

He felt as if he'd seen a girl running vigorously up the slope, her cardigan fluttering in the wind, but she blended into the darkness of the asphalt and quickly disappeared.

# CHAPTER 2

## GHOST AND WRITER

*A pickpocket girl and a wage-stealing miner, riding on a cart, set out on a big mining adventure. Will they escape the clutches of the rock monsters that come after them, make it to the deepest part of the mine, and find the legendary jewel?*

*An old miner tells his friends of the adventures of his youth in the second chapter of this popular series!*

The line of publicity caught her eye, and Kieli rested her hand a bit from wiping the counter and peered at the wrinkled newspaper someone had left there.

When she was in Easterbury, "newspaper" had meant the thoroughly boring periodical published by the branch of the Church there, but here it meant the biweekly paper put out by a miners' association in South-hairo that mainly published the state of the mining industry and news of miners' deaths.

"*It's a serial novel,*" came a whisper from the speaker of the radio sitting on a corner of the counter, blending with low-volume stringed musical instruments. Kieli looked up from the counter and shifted her gaze to the grumpy profile of the large man washing pots in the kitchen.

It was an old newspaper that had been wrapped around the pasta she'd brought out from the back of the cupboard. Kieli was about to throw it away when Buzz suddenly noticed it and took it from her. He would take a look at it in the evening when he had a little free time.

He didn't seem at all the type to read novels (although that was an unfair assumption), but thinking she had an excuse to talk to the normally silent Buzz, Kieli asked over the counter, "Is this any good?"

"No. It's third-rate."

Kieli was left without a response. His answer was brief and discouraged further conversation. Dealing with Buzz, she could almost convince herself that maybe Harvey was not gruff or untalkative at all but actually normal and easy to talk to.

"Oh, that? One of our old regulars wrote it," Suzie offered, looking up from her bookkeeping at the table in the corner. "But there were complaints from the association about the main characters or something, and it got discontinued after just two chapters. He was depressed for a while, and he would cry when he came here for dinner."

According to Suzie, Buzz had groveled, begging her to marry him, but no matter how hard she tried, Kieli could not imagine *that* Buzz ever doing anything of the sort. Suzie often told this story to customers, but Kieli didn't think a single one of them believed it.

"But I hear that lately he was able to sell an article to a magazine. It's one of those ideological magazines that's hard to read, so I don't know a thing about it, but rumor has it, he has quite an influence."

"That's incredible."

"It does sound incredible, doesn't it? But he suddenly stopped coming after that...," Suzie said, sounding a little lonely, as she closed her books and put everything in order.

"Hmm, I see..." was about all Kieli could muster in reaction, and Suzie turned a soft smile toward her.

"Business is slow today. Let's close early. Will you go clean up outside?"

"Yes, ma'am."

Kieli nodded and left the counter, heading for the door at a trot. Today was Sunday, and with no miners coming and going, it had been relatively empty all day. Around sunset, the customers stopped coming altogether. It didn't bother Suzie. She was of the opinion that it was nice to have days like this— they made life easier.

When Kieli pushed open the glass door, she heard the dry jingling of a bell overhead. The sun had set, and she huddled her shoulders a little in the outdoor air as she looked casually at the passersby dotting the street while the lamps started coming on when she noticed a tall young man walking down the slope across the road.

"Ah, Harvey!" she called out hurriedly. If he was passing by the diner, he could have stopped in...or anyway, he certainly didn't have to walk on the other side of the street as if he was specifically avoiding it.

The youth stopped in his tracks in the middle of the slope and turned her way. For a second, he wore a strange look, as if maybe he hadn't wanted her to call out to him. But he immediately returned to his usual deadpan expression and meandered her way, his hands shoved in the pockets of his work pants.

The streets were still chilly these early spring nights, but Harvey didn't seem to care—he dressed haphazardly, with a long-sleeved shirt thrown artlessly over his tank top. His copper hair looked just a little blue as it caught the color of the night sky and the dull lamplight.

"Where are you going?"

"Just had some stuff to do." As usual, that was no answer whatsoever. Recently, his unfriendly treatment didn't irk Kieli so much as it made her sad. Maybe her feelings showed on her face. It was really only a little bit, but Harvey looked as though he regretted it and added, "I won't be out that late tonight."

"Would you like to eat dinner together before you go? I was just about to invite Kieli," interjected Suzie, appearing at the glass door, cane in hand, but by then, Harvey had erased his aspect again, as if it was a reflex.

He sent an emotionless glance Suzie's way and didn't say a word to her.

"See you later," he said to Kieli, then turned ninety degrees and walked off.

"Ah! Wait, Harvey...." Kieli immediately started after him, but stopped after one step. She glanced back at Suzie, then at Harvey's back as he walked indifferently away, then back at Suzie again.

Suzie shrugged jokingly, but with a hint of loneliness.

"Maybe he hates me."

"I'm sorry; he doesn't. No, he's always been like that, but he's been through a lot, so he's been even more like that lately. Usually he's a little better, but he is basically like that, but..."

Kieli tried incoherently to smooth things over, but Suzie managed a smile and said, "It's all right. It doesn't bother me. I can tell he's not a bad person, since you try so hard to cover for him."

"I'm sorry...."

She felt even worse having Suzie provide this escape for her, and Kieli bowed her head again, throwing a glance down the slope by which Harvey had departed. His tall frame had already disappeared past a turn in the road, and the lights that dotted the street cast their dull light onto the asphalt.

She was sure that Harvey hadn't avoided people so blatantly

before. He may have been a little (a lot) gruff, but he used to talk to people pretty normally and had never had bad manners.

The slight change came after the incident.

The faces of the *Sandwalker*'s sailors, whom she'd met on the Sand Ocean, and of their leader floated into her mind. She figured that said leader, Ol Han, was one of the people Harvey had put in the "pretty good" category, one of Harvey's few friends. And he had tried to sell Harvey to the Church.

Since then, something—something that was very weak inside Harvey to begin with—snapped. That's the feeling she got. As for what that "something" was, it was so vague she couldn't really describe it, but it might have been something like his connection to the world.

"Kieli, let's get this cleaned up," Suzie said brightly as Kieli gazed down the twilit hill road, somehow getting more depressed. She pulled herself together and chased after Suzie, who was going back into the diner. It occurred to Kieli to ask Buzz to teach her how to make pound cake sometime. At her birthday party (not that it was big enough to call it that), Harvey had actually eaten all of his share for once, so he probably liked it pretty well.

"Oh yeah," Suzie said, stopping suddenly in the doorway. Kieli followed suit, and Suzie turned back toward her.

"This isn't for the diner, but can I ask you a favor?"

"Yes," Kieli replied, nodding.

"Seeing Harvey just now reminded me of another person I'm worried out of my mind about. I'd like you to bring him something on your way home."

Suzie went through the glass door at a rather light, happy gait, despite all her muttering about how she couldn't stand watching young people these days for all the worry they caused. Kieli quietly let out a dry laugh and started after her, when someone said, "Huh? You're done for the day?"

She turned toward the voice and saw two men who appeared to be miners standing under the streetlights. She didn't know one of them, but the other was a regular customer who came for lunch almost every day, so she had spoken with him a few times.

"I'm sorry. We're closed for..."

"Huh?" The man Kieli didn't know suddenly let out a yelp. "I come back after a while, and here Giena's back!"

"That's not Giena; she's a part-timer here. Kieli, right?"

"Er, um, yes." Kieli gaped at the regular customer but nodded all the same.

"Not Giena, huh? Now that you mention it, Giena would be bigger now, wouldn't she?" the other man said, blinking in surprise. Kieli blinked, too, unable to grasp what was going on, and looked up at the regular customer questioningly.

"Oh, Giena's the daughter here." The man mumbled something to himself like, "Come to think of it, their names are kinda similar," then continued in a cheerful tone. "But she left. That's why the missus always wants to take care of whatever young kid she sees."

"Left...?"

"My, my, if you're going to talk behind someone's back, do it when they can't hear you," a voice broke in, causing Kieli to swallow the question she was about to ask.

Suzie was leaning against the glass door, her arms crossed with a bit of an angry look on her face. When Suzie made that face, she was very intimidating.

"H-hey there, Suzie. Good evening."

The two men ducked their heads in shame, but Suzie immediately chuckled and softened her attitude. "We were about to close, but I guess there's no helping it. You're hungry, aren't you?" She urged them inside with her usual bright voice, then looked at Kieli, who stood frozen in place, and smiled wryly as if to say, "Such bothers."

"I'm sorry, but can you help here a little longer?"

"Ah, yes, ma'am," Kieli answered, a little flustered, and ran back inside. This was the first time she'd heard anything about a daughter, and she wondered why the girl had left. She wanted to ask but thought better of it. Just like Kieli had her own problems to deal with, Suzie and Buzz must have had theirs, and she figured that, either way, her knowing about it wouldn't change anything.

She gazed at Suzie's back as she herded the men into the diner and thought about something else instead. Suzie didn't meddle exclusively with young people: Whether they were big old miners or anyone else, in Suzie's mind, maybe most people were "troublesome children."

When she finished work and went back to the apartment, Kieli didn't go directly to the third floor but stopped one floor below, on the second story.

Thinking about it, she had learned the faces of the diner's regular customers pretty well, but on the other hand, she'd had hardly any interaction with the other residents of her apartment building after having been there an entire month.

The most she had done was to either pass by silently or exchange nods with the people she met on the outside stairs.

That's why she only learned about the young man who supposedly lived in the apartment on the far end of the second floor for the first time when Suzie told her about him.

She stood in front of the door and rang the bell, and heard a cracked "beeeep" on the other side.

She waited a little while, but there was no sign of anyone coming to the door. She tilted her head and murmured, "Maybe he's not home."

"*The light was on in the window,*" came the voice from the radio around her neck, reminding her that she had indeed seen the light on when she looked up at the second floor as she passed by out front.

She rang the bell once more and waited again, but, as expected, there was no response.

She looked down at the cloth package she carried and sighed, "Oh, dear." She could still feel the warmth of the little pot of stew through the wrapping. The care package Suzie had charged her with contained a small pot of Buzz & Suzie's Café's famous poultry, egg, and chickpea parent-and-child stew and three rolls of Buzz's own special onion-and-corn bread.

Kieli looked up at the door that no one answered and found herself at a loss.

"I can't not give it to him...."

"*Can't you just eat it yourself?*"

"No, I can't. She asked me to give it to him." She puffed out her cheeks a little as she chided the radio for his irresponsible suggestion and tried the knob, figuring it wouldn't hurt to give it a shot. "Huh...?" It was unlocked.

She realized that she could just leave it in the entrance and go home, but even so, she got the feeling that she really shouldn't open the door without permission. Inwardly apologizing with, "I'm not anyone suspicious," she quietly opened the door and peered inside.

A light spilled in from the door to the room she saw at the other end of the gloomy hallway. She heard a faint, dry, crinkling sound, as if someone was tapping something.

Kieli relaxed. "So he is home." After a moment, though, she thought it might be a thief or something and got scared. She looked down at the radio and convinced herself that she would be fine because the Corporal was with her, then entered the hall with silent footsteps; it was then that she suddenly realized what she was doing.

*Erk, why did I come inside...?*

She'd meant to leave the package in the entryway and go home, but once she sensed people, she'd found herself venturing in.

By the time the thought occurred to her, Kieli was already peeking inside the room within from the doorway.

The ceiling light wasn't on, but a lamp from a desk stand lit the area around it under the window, creating one area of dim illumination in the center of the gloom. Kieli noticed someone sitting at the desk with his back to her and breathed a sigh of relief. Thieves probably wouldn't sit at desks, so it must be the person who lived here.

That thought was a little comforting, but then, wasn't that sure to put *her* in the position of thief now?

"Um, good evening," she said, realizing she really would be suspect if she stayed quiet.

The shadow at the desk twitched his shoulders a bit—she thought, but it may have only been her imagination. Just as she'd gotten no response from ringing the bell, he showed no sign of acknowledgment even after she waited a bit. Either he was so immersed in the work at his desk that he didn't notice her, or he did notice and was purposely ignoring her.

She looked over his shoulder to see what he was doing. He faced a typewriter on the desk and appeared to be giving his full attention to typing on it. Papers he had started typing on littered the floor around him.

After coming up with the absentminded impression, "He's like a writer!" she remembered that he really was a writer.

According to Suzie, the person living in this apartment was a young novelist and the author of the mining adventure story that was in the newspaper. She thought it might be kind of cool living in the same apartment building as someone who wrote stories for newspapers and magazines.

*I guess I shouldn't bother him....* Kieli pondered for a moment, looking down at the parcel with the stew. She thought about putting it down and leaving without a word, but she also got the feeling that, since he was here, it would be better for him to eat it while it was still warm.

"That's right." She nodded to herself, then approached the desk, taking care not to step on the papers strewn about the floor. She stopped behind the young man, took a breath, and called out in a louder voice than before, "Excuse me, hello!" This time she got a reaction—too much of a reaction.

The man suddenly lifted his head and turned around, abruptly shouting "Quiet!" But more than the outburst, his features startled Kieli, and she instinctively leapt backward.

She landed on a piece of paper on the floor, and her heel slipped. She let out a little scream and fell on her rear end, kicking papers up as she went, and realized a second too late that she had let go of the parcel she had been holding. The package was flung to the floor, and its wrapping came undone; the stewpot flipped over, and the bread tumbled out.

She stared in terror at the milky stain spreading across the floor and automatically let out a sigh. She might have looked very much like she was about to cry.

Kieli timidly lifted her gaze to check the man's expression. He stood frozen, half out of his chair, looking, as she was, down at the disaster on the floor; but when his eyes met Kieli's, he panicked, jumped out of his chair, and ran to her.

"I-I'm sorry for yelling. Are you okay?"

He crouched down and picked up the small pot, then looked around hurriedly, as if at a loss for how to deal with the spilled liquid.

"Ah, I'm all right...."

She gaped up at the youth's features, and felt just a little disappointed. His face had been unbelievably terrifying and twisted a second before, but maybe she had imagined it. There was nothing scary about him anymore. He did seem somewhat jumpy, but overall, the slender-faced young man appeared mild-mannered. She could kind of understand why seeing Harvey would remind Suzie of him. They both appeared slender and delicate—but while Harvey was just really thin, the man before her looked emaciated. He had hollow cheeks and sunken eyes, and his complexion was ashen—the picture of poor health.

"Is this stew from Buzz & Suzie's Café?" the man asked in a

listless, tired voice as he started to wipe the mess with a nearby shirt that had been abandoned on the floor after it was taken off. Thinking it would be better not to use such a thing to mop the floor, Kieli picked up the bread that had rolled across it.

"Yes. I'm working there now. And Suzie asked me to bring this to you, but no one came to the door, so…" *I just came in.*

"Suzie still remembers me. I appreciate that."

"She was worried because you haven't been to the diner lately. Um, are you getting enough to eat?" When she saw how obviously worn out the young man was, even Kieli started to worry about him, and she had never met him before.

"Oh, that's not important. I'm really on a roll in my writing right now," the man answered with a broad smile, turning back to his desk.

That instant, Kieli felt a chill and backed away in spite of herself.

Deep in his haggard eye sockets, the youth's eyes glinted oddly as he gazed at the typewriter on his desk. She thought he meant to smile, but the corners of his mouth twisted strangely.

"That's right, I have to write…."

He staggered up and returned to his desk, stretching his hands in front of him as if trying to grab something invisible in the air. He practically crawled back into his chair and faced his typewriter, then started pounding the keys again.

"Um, what should I do with this…?" Kieli asked the youth's back, confused that he'd abandoned her in the middle of the cleanup. They had just been conversing a minute ago, but now the man clung to the typewriter and battered away at the keys, as if he'd forgotten all about Kieli in the blink of an eye.

"Um…"

*"Kieli, get outside,"* she suddenly heard the radio whisper. *"Get out of here. Now."*

She looked blankly down at the radio, and when she returned her gaze to the young man, something long and thin was sticking out of the typewriter.

It was a human arm.

"……!"

Kieli groped at the floor behind her and jumped half a meter backward. Two arms wrapped around the man's back, followed by the arms' owner, crawling out onto the desk—a thin man, enveloped in a black shadow. The youth didn't even blink as he kept hitting the keys.

Once he had sluggishly pulled the top half of his body out of the typewriter, the shadow's gaze swiveled toward Kieli. Under the dull light from the desk stand, a twisted grin, just like the one the youth had smiled a moment ago, rose to his cheeks. As if in response, the scattered papers on the floor danced up and started to swirl in the air.

*"Kieli, get up! Get out of here!"*

With the sharp command, Kieli felt a forceful impact against her abdomen, and at the same time a mass of air flew from the radio's speaker. The shock wave dispersed the paper vortex, and white papers danced all over the room, blocking her field of vision.

Kieli gasped and flipped over, then dashed out of the room, practically on all fours. She sprinted down the hall, tripping over her feet and nearly falling as she went, and turned the doorknob, clinging to it with both hands, then burst through

the door and rushed into the outside hall. Immediately afterward, the door slammed shut behind her.

"Wha...!?"

She sank to the ground in the hall outside and timidly turned her head behind her, out of breath.

"What was that...?"

She felt as though she could still hear the dry sound of typing on the other side of the door. The image of the youth's back as he pounded away at the keys under the light of the desk lamp, drifting like a solitary island in the gloom, stuck to her retinas for a while and wouldn't go away.

"Forget about him."

When she told Harvey (who ended up not coming back until after midnight despite having said he wouldn't be out late that night) about the young man on the second floor, he answered with the line she had predicted would be his most likely response.

Although she had anticipated it, Kieli still faltered unhappily; Harvey sat down at his usual post on the sofa, pulled out a cigarette, and said, "If it's like the Corporal's telling me, he's big trouble."

"*This isn't just a little spirit possession. This is a nasty, evil spirit that pulls in people's hearts and controls them,*" the radio added, sitting next to the sofa, and Harvey nodded.

"This isn't something you can do anything about just because you kind of feel like it."

"But…that's why I'm talking to you, Harvey."

"Huh?" Harvey asked and looked up, his lighter still lit in front of his cigarette. His face was honestly, genuinely blank. "Why should I have to do anything for him?" he demanded bluntly, his voice a little muffled because of the cigarette in his mouth.

"Why? Because…" Kieli couldn't come up with a continuation for the sentence.

"…Kieli."

Harvey breathed a short sigh as he looked down and went back to lighting his cigarette.

"I'm serious. Stop sticking your nose where it doesn't belong because you're curious or because you like to meddle."

"I don't just 'kind of feel like it….'" Kieli pouted and tried to argue.

"Shut up and listen," he commanded in an unexpectedly sharp tone, so she closed her mouth.

After a minute of silence, Harvey slowly exhaled the smoke he had inhaled. "Look. I'm not talking about you; *I* don't like it. I would really hate it if you got in trouble and I didn't know about it," he said in a low voice, and didn't say another word for the rest of the day.

Still, Harvey thought he was a pretty appallingly softhearted guy, himself. After living so many years, it was only recently that he'd finally realized that.

"I may not look it, but I'm busy with stuff, you know."

*"What kind of 'stuff'?"*

"…Stuff," he answered vaguely, then averted his eyes from the radio hanging from his hand and looked up at the flock of laundry swaying overhead. Laundry lines straddled the path from the windows of the buildings lining either side of the narrow hill road just off Mine Street, and white shirts and sheets fluttered peacefully in the breeze (although they'd probably turn gray the minute a three-wheeled bike rode through).

It was a warm afternoon in early spring, with a relatively low concentration of the umber-colored gas covering the sky. He descended the slanting road, slightly avoiding the occasional passerby. He did get the feeling there was something off about two men's voices talking in whispers under such a pleasant sky.

*"I've been keeping quiet because Kieli doesn't want to bug you about it, but seriously, what are you doing?"*

"Something personal. I'll tell her about it soon enough."

*"Damn it, what's that supposed to mean!?"*

"Quiet. Don't talk so loud," Harvey ordered the radio, which had started to raise its voice, and looked around instinctively, but that wasn't necessarily the action that helped him find the sign he had been looking for down the road.

"Oh, there it is."

He stopped walking in front of a single shop standing in the middle of the slope. A rusty sign hung from a door so low it appeared half sunken into the ground. The street was bright and sunny in the spring weather, but a strangely heavy, shady atmosphere wafted around that door.

Apparently this was the one and only antique store in town that dealt with typewriters—in this day and age, antique shops were the only place you could get typewriters to begin with. In cities with communications technology, information terminals were used for dealing with the written word.

The knob had some kind of engraving on it that was so worn it was impossible to tell what it was anymore. Harvey grabbed it and pulled. As he winced at the clatter made by the ill-fitting door, he was accosted by a sudden shout.

"Go away!"

He automatically turned and almost left, but it seemed that the conversation in the back of the shop was not directed at him.

It was a small, gloomy store, permeated with the smell of dust. Miscellaneous objects crammed the shelves on either side in a jumbled mess, and in the very back, there was a counter similarly packed with things, to the point where it hardly fulfilled its proper function at all.

He saw a man who appeared to be the shopkeeper on the far side of the counter, and on the near side of the counter, a small man stood facing him. They seemed to be having a heated discussion, but the shopkeeper noticed Harvey and turned his way.

"Ah, a customer, is it!? Come in!"

He plastered a businesslike smile to his cheeks and leaned over the counter, shoving the first customer aside.

"No, I'm not really a customer."

"Hey, I'm not done talking to—"

"You just go home already." The conversation jumbled together in the already cluttered shop, muddling the air even further, and Harvey was seriously starting to want to leave.

"Oh! Could that be—" the shopkeeper suddenly shouted

excitedly. He addressed Harvey with a friendly smile, but still watched him as if appraising him. Then his grin broadened to a point where it was actually creepy.

"I know what you're here for, sir. Please, please, come inside."

"......?"

He put his guard up just in case and accepted the invitation to go inside. The shopkeeper leaned so far over the counter that he looked as if he would fall over it and peered at the radio.

"Oh, I knew it. This...I'm surprised anyone would have such a thing...."

He sighed dreamily, took a pen out of his breast pocket, and started writing numbers on a notepad.

"Three hundred...four hundred, no, I'll give you four-fifty. What do you think? If it weren't so beat up, I wouldn't go under seven hundred, but, well, there are some buyers who like them beat up; say it gives them more flavor."

"Er, uh. Wait a second."

At last Harvey figured out there was some kind of a misunderstanding. "I'm not here to sell this." Just as he thought for a fleeting moment that if the price was right he might consider it, the other customer who had been pushed aside came to stare at the radio with a fascination not to be outdone by the shopkeeper's.

When Harvey saw the customer, his jaw dropped a little. He was a small man whose age was hard to guess—the white mixed with his hair and the deep wrinkles at the corners of his eyes made him look old, but his facial features made him look young. The patron created an impression that was difficult to explain, but the most unusual thing of all was the black monocle placed over his left eye, as if it was eating into the socket. It wasn't a small one like they use at watch shops, but half of a pair of night-vision goggles from the War era, cut off and stuck onto his eye.

Harvey looked down at the grotesque monocle and unconsciously froze. With no warning gesture, the man stuck out his hands and grabbed hold of the radio.

"Ack, what the hell?" Harvey immediately brushed him away, but the man remained undaunted.

"Hey, let me have it. Let me have it."

"*Erk....*" Maybe having this strange man caress him shook the Corporal up. A voice leaked out of the speaker. Harvey winced a little himself and gulped. *What the hell...?*

And then the man looked up from the radio and now, suddenly, turned his eyes on Harvey. He let out a sigh of some unknown meaning, then the lens of his monocle moved from the top of Harvey's head to the tip of his toes, as if lapping him up.

"You!"

He suddenly grabbed Harvey's arm.

"Uwah!" Harvey cried out automatically and pulled away.

"Cut it out! Don't do weird things to my customers!" The shopkeeper picked up a duster and started brandishing it wildly. "I thought I told you to go away! Go on, go home!" The duster drove the monocled man off, and he fled the shop, wailing.

"Hmph! Damn your shop to bankruptcy!" he spat nonsensically before turning around and escaping, followed by the shopkeeper's jeers of: "Don't you ever come back. The next time I see you here, I'm turning you over to the Watch!" He yanked the door violently open and slammed it shut. The consequent wind sent dust dancing through the air.

When the bizarre customer had gone and the dust had settled back to the floor, a strangely awkward silence fell over the shop.

"Honestly. Sorry about that weird guy." The shopkeeper came back after tossing the duster to its place by the wall. "He's a freak who's taken up residence in the ruins outside town. He doesn't have any money, but he used to come all the time, wanting the typewriter I had here until a little while ago. I chased him out every time he showed up. I told him I sold it to someone else, but he keeps hanging around, trying to find out who I sold it to."

"Actually, I came here to talk about that typewriter. Do you know anything about it at all, like who it used to belong to?" Harvey asked, placing his elbow on the counter. It was convenient that the topic he wanted to discuss had just come up.

"Don't tell me you're in league with that freak, sir...."

The shopkeeper furrowed his brow suspiciously. Harvey hurriedly shook his head, and, while he was at it, switched the elbow he was leaning on from his right to his left and shoved his right hand in his pocket. He didn't like to admit it, but he was in the same category as the monocled man, in the sense that they both had unusual machines stuck to them.

On the other side of the counter, the shopkeeper also put his elbow on the counter and leaned forward.

"It's a ludicrous story, but, well, think of it as a good conversation starter," he prefaced, then deliberately lowered his voice and began. "Its previous owner and the one before that both wore themselves out and died. The typewriter's first owner was a celebrated author, but apparently he wrote works that profaned the Church, and they had him executed. They say that ever since then, the author has possessed the typewriter and is moving around the South-hairo continent, sacrificing one owner after another, so he can complete the masterpiece he was never able to finish...."

He broke off there and peered into Harvey's eyes as if he wanted to say something.

"What?"

"You're not scared?"

"Not really," Harvey replied indifferently.

The shopkeeper pulled his face away, as if his fun had suddenly been spoiled. "But everyone pretty much believes it."

"What? You made it up?" It wasn't as if Harvey didn't believe him.

"Well, *I* didn't make it up. I mean, it's stupid, isn't it? A vengeful spirit possessing a typewriter," he said flatly, unaware that there was a possessed radio right in front of his eyes.

*Doesn't look like hearing any more of this will help,* Harvey determined and quickly left the counter.

"Sorry to bother you. Bye."

"Sir, are you sure you don't want to sell that radio? I'll give you five hundred for it." The man's voice followed him, as if reluctant to see him go, so Harvey stopped for a moment. He looked down at the radio and thought for a bit, then turned to the shopkeeper, a serious look on his face, and said, "Five-fifty."

"Done."

Immediately afterward, a shock wave flew from the radio, destroying a shelf and creating an avalanche of the piles of goods it had been carrying, and Harvey ended up having to flee the shop at lightning speed while the shopkeeper fell into a panic.

Buzz & Suzie's Café was busy on Mondays. There were a lot of customers, and lots of foodstuffs arrived from the market, so Buzz and Suzie had to prepare and put away ingredients, keeping an eye on the diner all the while. As a result, they spent the entire day on their feet.

So it wasn't until late in the afternoon, when the customers had finally started to thin out, that Suzie asked, "How did it go yesterday?"

*He looked fine. He ate the food and said it was delicious.* That's what Kieli wanted to say, but while there were a lot of things that she couldn't say, she didn't want to lie to Suzie. Instead, she spoke honestly about the part where she'd flipped over the pot of stew. The look of dejection on Suzie's face hurt her chest.

After that, Suzie took on all of Kieli's work herself, thus managing to let Kieli off half an hour early, and sent her off with another care package, as well as an order to collect the pot from the day before.

And that's why Kieli was once again standing in front of the door at the far end of the hall on the second floor, holding another package.

She had been standing stock-still for five minutes, at a complete and total loss.

Kieli was worried about the young man from yesterday, too,

and she wanted to help Suzie. But she didn't want to make Harvey unhappy.

After fretting over it, she prioritized what was most important to her, and the solution came relatively easily.

*...I'm not going to do this.*

She had better not do anything reckless on her own, at least until Harvey got back. The Corporal had given Harvey a hard time, saying that even if he told Kieli to leave it alone, in the end, she wouldn't be able to anyway. So he had gone off to investigate the typewriter.

*Yeah, I'm going home.*

When she spun around and started to leave the door behind, she heard a sound from inside.

She stopped and turned back to the door. She thought about how she shouldn't worry about it—she had decided to go home. She could just ask Harvey and get him to come with her to check it out later. She got the feeling that the noise she heard was the sound of something big falling over. It wasn't as if she heard anything else after that; the sound just stopped completely. *What happened? But I'm not going to worry about it; I'm going home.*

*...What if he's dead?*

The thought floated to her head, and she opened the door.

Just like yesterday, the desk lamp leaked out of the room at the end of the gloomy hall. She fixed her gaze on it, crouched down, and left the package at the entrance. Then she stepped inside and peered into the room from the doorway.

"A-are you all right!?"

She immediately saw the young man lying facedown on the floor, as if he'd slipped out of his chair.

She ran over to help him up. When she looked into his face, her jaw dropped. He was much more emaciated than he had been the day before. It was hard to believe only a day had passed.

"Oh, you're the girl from yesterday. I'm all right...," came a weak voice that sounded far from all right. The youth ran his glazed yellow eyes unsteadily around the room, stopping when they found the typewriter on top of the desk. He clung to the chair and tried to force himself up.

"No! You have to rest a little...."

"Leave me alone!"

He pushed her away roughly, and Kieli staggered once but immediately stood up, moved in front of the young man, and reached out to the typewriter. That instant, the youth's cheeks twisted in rage. "Don't touch it!"

"If you keep going like this, you'll die!"

"Give it back!" They each grabbed hold of the typewriter and struggled to take it from the other.

At this point, Kieli had more physical strength. The young man tottered and fell. She took the opportunity to snatch the typewriter away—

The window. Her first thought was to open the window.

"Stop! What are you doing!?"

She held it over her head and was about to throw it out the window, but the youth grabbed her clothes and pulled her to the floor. Even so, she tried to reach out to the typewriter as it rolled across the floor when she let out a gasp of pain.

She didn't know what had happened, but her breath stopped for a second. It was after she had rolled to the wall that she realized he had kicked her in the side, and she doubled over and coughed as she regained her breath.

She caught the youth's figure at the edge of her vision. He embraced the typewriter in both hands, held it to his cheek, and stroked the casing lovingly. Watching the scene of madness with her cheek still on the floor, Kieli shuddered and stiffened. Just then, the shadow of a man crawled out of the typewriter like it had done the day before.

The shadow glared at her, wearing the same features— twisted and full of insanity—as the young man. At the same time, the papers littering the floor rustled and danced upward. As Kieli watched, they formed a white tornado and started swirling around her.

She felt a twinge of pain on the back of her hand and looked at it in surprise; a thin line of blood rose out of it. There was a sharp *fwip* and another line of blood....

"No...!" She covered her head with both arms and huddled on the floor, when—

*Crash!*

She heard a spectacular breaking sound, and the wind stirring up the papers suddenly vanished.

As she crouched on the ground, white sheets fluttered at the edge of her vision, floating down like giant confetti. She looked up, still holding her head, and saw long legs in familiar work pants standing a little ahead of her.

The typewriter fell out of the small dent it had made in the room's opposite wall, along with some pieces of the wall itself. It came apart and its pieces scattered onto the floor. Apparently he had kicked it across the room.

"Ah...aaauughh..." A strangled, anguished cry came from the young man's mouth. He crawled along the floor and tried to snuggle up to the typewriter, but Harvey's shoe trampled his side.

"Huh...?"

Kieli looked up in surprise, then immediately swallowed her voice. As Harvey looked down at the youth, his profile was so perfectly void of expression that it made her shudder. No emotion on his face, but rage burning in his copper eyes, he kicked the young man again and again. The youth curled up and let out a weak scream.

"Harvey, stop! What are you doing? Stop it!"

She couldn't quite stand up, so Kieli practically crawled as she rushed over. "You can't! He's just a human being! He'll die!" she begged frantically, clinging to his torso. Harvey looked as if he suddenly came to his senses and stopped immediately.

"Ah..."

After standing frozen in that position for a time, he turned to face her, his movements somehow sluggish. "... Well, but—" He started to make excuses as he returned his attention to the young man trembling and cowering on the floor. "He... kicked you," Harvey murmured in a slightly dazed voice, as if he didn't quite understand it himself.

After that, the youth ate all of Suzie's care package, crying and apologizing all the while. He got a good night's sleep, and the next morning, he packed up a few things and headed for the station. When Kieli asked him if he was sure he wasn't going to go see Suzie, he answered that he would leave without seeing her, because if she saw him like this, it would only worry her more.

Looking at him, Kieli didn't see a single trace of the previous night's insanity. It had been only a day, so of course he was still haggard and emaciated, but a smile rose to his mild-mannered, slender face.

"I haven't been back home in a long while. I'll recuperate a little while I think of what I'm going to do next." He looked a little sad even as he said it.

Apparently he'd left his parents in his hometown and come to this city when his first story was published in a newspaper, but he was soon out of work and couldn't even go back home. That's when he got the typewriter. It was a mysterious appliance—all he had to do was hit the keys, and eloquent writing flowed out of it. He kept writing as if possessed, thinking that *this time* he would succeed, but when he thought about it rationally, the young man realized that that story definitely did not come from inside himself.

"I liked that mining story. I hope I can read the rest someday," said Kieli. She had taken the old newspaper home out of curiosity and found herself unexpectedly hooked. When she gave him her honest opinion, the youth smiled happily.

"Would you like to have an adventure like that?" he asked, making small talk. Kieli thought for a bit, then dodged the question with a vague nod.

She saw the young man off and left the station, then climbed the hill on the three-wheeled bike she'd borrowed from the diner.

"*Well, it is a little late for that. Your life story is already pretty unique,*" the radio said sarcastically, hanging from her neck. Kieli looked down at it and pouted.

"I do think it's because I hang out with you and Harvey, Corporal."

"Well, excuse me for being unique," a careless voice jumped in from the backseat. She glanced over her shoulder to see Harvey's profile, cigarette in his mouth.

Since the three-wheeled bike had a fuel tank that was extremely large for the vehicle's size in the back, the backseat on top of it was inevitably large as well. Still, she thought it might be pretty dangerous to crouch on top of it, facing sideways and smoking. Kieli wouldn't have minded sitting in the back herself, but apparently Harvey had no desire to drive.

*I don't like it*—Harvey didn't say a word about how she'd completely trampled over his statement from two nights before and ended up going to the neighbor's room alone after all. He didn't seem mad; he just looked down at the light cuts on Kieli's hand and made a face that she couldn't really interpret. It might have been his "I don't like it" face.

Anyway, the one thing that Kieli thought emphatically was that she couldn't let him make that face again.

The front of Buzz & Suzie's Café came into view at the top of the slope. It was a relief to confirm from far off that there were no customers at the outside tables. When she'd explained the situation to Suzie, she'd gotten permission to go see the youth off, and she was glad to get back before the diner got busy.

Getting close to her destination, she slowed down and pulled over to the side of the road.

*"So what happened to the typewriter?"*

"He told me it was broken, so he threw it away," she answered, focusing on her driving.

"It wasn't there," Harvey interjected simply from behind her.

"What?" She found herself slamming on the brakes. The bike screeched against the asphalt as it came to a sudden stop, and Harvey, almost thrown off the backseat, yelped and clung to Kieli.

"That freaked me out. Watch it!"

"It's because you were sitting like that," Kieli argued, her heart skipping a beat at the closeness of his voice and the feeling of his arms around her torso. "What do you mean it wasn't there?"

She hurried to get back on the subject, thinking he might feel her heartbeat in his arms. For his part, it didn't seem to bother Harvey, who said in his usual tone, "It wasn't in the trash heap. I went to check it out this morning, but the typewriter wasn't there. Maybe somebody picked it up."

"What would they do with it?"

"Hell if I know. Probably use it, or fix it and sell it."

"But if it possesses someone again…"

"I don't care," Harvey said shortly, then let go of her and got off the bike. He stretched a little on the curb, and mused, "What's wrong with having a few pieces of junk like that out in the world? There's one right there."

"*Don't treat me like junk! You almost sold me for five-fifty!*" the radio growled accusingly, then Kieli heard a smart little jingle up the road, and a small woman appeared by the glass door to Buzz & Suzie's Café.

"Welcome back. Thanks for seeing him off."

Suzie worked her cane busily as she hurried toward them. Apparently it bothered her that she couldn't go see the young man off herself. "I'll be at home," Harvey whispered and started to leave. Suzie didn't fail to notice.

"Wait, wait. Today you *will* be eating before you leave!"

"Why are you so damn persistent...?" he muttered in a voice Suzie couldn't hear, but his annoyance showed clearly in his attitude as he stopped walking. Suzie didn't care in the slightest and grabbed his arm as if to say she wouldn't let him escape this time. That instant, her eyes and mouth opened wide.

"You really *are* thin! Are you eating? You aren't, are you? You have to eat properly!"

"It's none of your business...." Harvey shook off her hand, halfway between furious and polite, as though it was a little too much for him.

"Ah!"

"Ah—" Kieli cried out automatically, her voice overlapping Suzie's. Suzie's cane missed the ground, and she staggered forward.

Kieli already had her hands out, but before they could reach Suzie, Harvey's arm caught the woman.

Immediately after, he let go and looked away, apparently inwardly cursing his mistake, but Suzie, still wrapping her arms around Harvey's, smiled happily. "I knew you were a good person. Right, Kieli?"

Kieli answered with a shy smile and a nod in the affirmative.

# CHAPTER 3

BUMPING HEADS ON WEDNESDAY,
MISSING EACH OTHER ON THURSDAY

"Beatrice."

Whenever someone called her that, she would either correct them immediately or, when she was in a bad mood, ignore them. Well, "Beatrice" was better than the alternative; she had one old acquaintance that called her by the insanely abbreviated nickname "Bea," but she had given up on that man long ago.

Anyway, she wasn't in a bad mood today, so she corrected, "Beatrix."

"Oh, right, right. You're just as pretty as ever today, Beatrice."

As she wasn't tolerant enough to correct him a second time, she ignored him, but maybe the man didn't realize he was being ignored. He laughed a hiccup of a laugh and cheerfully gulped down his glass of diluted whiskey. *Destroy your liver and retire already, you drunk,* she cursed inwardly, but she would lose everything if he retired today. For the time being, she kept her abusive comments to herself.

Beatrix listened with half an ear as he kept talking about a vicious criminal who had holed himself up with a stolen carbonization gun, and how he caught the felon after a shoot-out, garnering a public acknowledgment from the Church. She paid no attention and brought the cigarette she had been toying with to her lips. It was a slender, scented cigarette. When lit, it gave off a sharp, spicy fragrance. Beatrix didn't smoke these cigarettes because she liked the scent. In fact, she more or less hated it. The stuffy air in the hall was bad enough to make her sick, though, and they helped her distract herself just a tiny bit, so she always smoked this brand at work.

Through the scented tobacco smoke, she surveyed the hall, clouded with purple smoke and the stench of alcohol. One or two female employees sat at each table under the dim lights, serving alcohol to customers, and not hesitating to drink from their own glasses as well. Well, that was the point of this place. Most of the customers were from the Watch, and it had the feel of an establishment that catered to the Watch.

"The Watch" referred to organizations of citizens that existed only in the towns of South-hairo parish. This continent had managed to avoid a fair amount of the ravages of the great War in the past, so the Church didn't intervene in the name of reconstruction, and even now, the garrisons of Church Soldiers were stationed only at the main ports. Instead, they built up city organizations for public order—but either way, the leaders of those organizations were connected to the Church.

And Beatrix believed that the Watch was the most good-for-nothing group in town. It was a gathering of bums who hated the steady work of mining and had dropped out.

The second-in-command sitting next to her was in the bums' middle management, and putting it that way made him seem much more like a bum. Still, he was useful in his own way. Today in particular, she needed him to act as the middleman between herself and her goal.

*Now then, it should almost be time....*

The shop door opened, and new customers appeared, just as her advance information had said they would. The dry night wind blew in, lightly stirring the stagnant air of the hall.

The cigarette still in the corner of her mouth, Beatrix threw a casual glance their way and watched. They were a large man and a slender fellow in black robes. The big one was the chief of the Watch, and she had seen him a few times before. This was the first time she had seen the one in the robes, but he was the one she urgently wanted to talk to.

"Say, do you know him?" she asked the man beside her, watching as the newcomers were greeted politely and escorted to a table inside. The man, who had switched topics to something like the hardships of middle management, broke off in disappointment.

"Oh, it's the chief! I need to go see if he's in a good mood... I mean, go say hello!"

"Not him, the other one. In the robes." Her companion had scuttled up from his seat, and she held him back for a moment.

Half standing, he tilted his head and followed her gaze. "Oh, I know him. He's the adviser to the parish's chief priest. I hear he used to be the close aide to the chief priest in Westerbury."

"Huh," she murmured casually, pressed her still-long cigarette into the ashtray, and stood up from her chair. The man sent a curious glance her way, so she said, "You're going to say hello, aren't you? Will you introduce me?"

She said it with a bright smile, but actually, she felt a little panic on the inside. A priest's aide from Westerbury—she had a bit of a history with Westerbury. It might be dangerous to talk to him. But that was a long time ago, and she didn't think they had her face on record.

This was a request from an old friend she hadn't seen in a while, and while she had happily agreed to do it, things seemed to be getting dicey.

*Well, there's no helping it; I can go out of my way to help him. I do owe him....*

She braced herself, plastered on a flawless professional smile, and approached the two men's table. The second-in-command spoke quickly, flattering the chief and the priest, then urged her forward.

"This is Beatrice—"

"Beatrix. It's an honor to meet you." She curtsied elegantly and took the opportunity to stomp on the second-in-command's foot.

"He has red hair, he's about college age, he's tall and thin, his right arm is prosthetic, and he kinda seems like he's unsteady on his feet, but he walks fast.... Have you seen someone like that?" Kieli rattled, doing her best to list all the features that came to mind and thinking that with such a jumbled explanation they probably wouldn't know it even if they *had* seen him. But surprisingly, the message seemed to get through, and the person said, "Oh, I saw him," and told her about a shop at the end of the alley. Harvey probably didn't like it, but whatever he might say, he stood out a great deal, looking the way he did.

"Thank you very much," she told the friendly person, then twisted the accelerator of the three-wheeled bike and drove slowly down the alley.

*"I feel like we've done this before."*

"Yeah, me too...," Kieli agreed with the radio's voice and added to herself, *But it was the Corporal's idea to follow him both times. It wasn't me.*

The curtain of night was beginning to fall over the narrow line of sky she saw through a gap in the buildings of the alley. The gray smoke that spewed from the exhaust pipes protruding from the buildings' roofs reflected the last rays of sunlight as they melted into the sky.

It was Wednesday, the middle of the week, and the business district downtown had begun to bustle with miners on their way home from work. Kieli had been on her way back after delivering something for Suzie when she caught sight of a copper-colored head at the district's entrance, and immediately the radio had said, *"All right, let's follow him!"*

"Um, hey, well, I am curious about what he's doing, but I trust Harvey and don't want to push too hard trying to find out."

*"I don't doubt him either. It's not like he's doing anything he should feel guilty about. He doesn't have those kinds of lusts."* He added that that wasn't a compliment. Kieli was just a little puzzled at what he meant by "those kinds of lusts."

"Then why are we following him?"

*"... Why indeed?"*

"......" Kieli felt like throwing the radio.

*"Don't worry about it; it's just a habit. We'll just check on him and leave."*

When she got out of the alley, she stopped the bike and looked up at the entrance to the place she had been directed to. A rusty, but thick and heavy, iron door blended into the night street. A man who appeared to be a miner came from across the road and stopped right in front of the door, opening it and gazing at her somewhat questioningly. She took advantage and peered inside.

"Erk..."

Kieli faltered for a second at the chokingly stagnant air.

At the end of her field of vision, fully obscured by billows of yellow smoke, she could see a dimly lit hall down half a flight of stairs. Round tables of varying sizes stood at narrow intervals, and customers sat around them, amusing themselves with card games.

"A gambling house...," she found herself muttering in disappointment.

In a similar voice, the radio said, "*Aww, he's just doing the same stuff as always!*" Kieli was thinking something along those same lines, though she wouldn't say it so bluntly. Well, the one time she'd asked him where he was going, he had answered with, "Cards," so it was completely selfish of them to feel deflated just because he hadn't been lying.

"Let's go home...."

She was backing away, still peering into the hall, when she bumped into a customer who came in after her and lurched forward. Almost falling, she ran down a few steps, then clung to the wall and stopped. "Oops, sorry," the customer behind her apologized casually, then gave her a dubious glance and descended into the hall.

A fifteen-year-old girl who worked part-time at a café must have seemed out of place here. Although it would be a little better if she was with Harvey.

She started to feel very uncomfortable. She plastered herself to the stairway wall, still hiding, and found herself peering into the hall to see if she could find a copper-colored head somewhere.

"Huh...?"

She couldn't find a copper one, but instead she found a gold-colored head—a woman with gentle waves of long blond hair, alone at a small table by the wall. She sat so that the beauty of her legs showed through the deep slit in her long skirt, resting her chin on her hand and taking a drink. "Corporal, that woman. Look, over there," Kieli whispered a bit excitedly.

Immediately after, she instinctively held her breath and froze.

A tall silhouette approached the woman's table—a young man with copper hair. He placed the ashtray he was carrying on the table, sat across from the woman, and pulled a cigarette out of his pack with the corner of his mouth. When he set the pack on the table, the woman helped herself to one, and the man looked annoyed but didn't say anything as they put their faces together and lit their cigarettes with one lighter. They started to talk, their faces still close enough to touch.

Kieli still clung to the wall and stared at the table, temporarily paralyzed. She came to her senses when she heard the sound of the bike's key that she had been holding fall to the ground, and a meaningless little sound escaped her throat. Her voice was low enough to blend in with the clamor inside, but just then the woman happened to look her way, and her blue eyes met Kieli's.

The woman opened her mouth in surprise, and the young man noticed and turned to look—then made a face that clearly showed he knew he was in trouble. After a pause, he jumped out of his chair. Instinctively, Kieli turned and tried to run, but when she picked up the key, dropped it, and picked it up again, he caught her arm from behind.

She gulped and went rigid for a second, then turned her head jerkily back, lifting her gaze up along her captured arm.

"You…!" Harvey started to say, then closed his mouth for a moment, opening it again a second later. "What are you doing here?" He said it in his normal tone, but Kieli could sense some panic mixed in.

"N-nothing. I saw you and wondered where you were going, so..."

"...You followed me."

"...Yeah." She dropped her head, peering up at him through her eyelashes.

"Oh, man...," Harvey breathed with a sigh.

"*Don't you 'oh, man' me! What the hell are you—*" the radio started to interject, but immediately went quiet, leaving behind some grumpy static. A clear woman's voice came from over Harvey's shoulder.

"This is a surprise. So this girl is an acquaintance of yours?"

"Acquaintance? Something like that...," Harvey answered vaguely, looking back at the woman, then questioned her instead: "Hey, how do *you* know her?" Although Kieli did get the feeling he may also have been dodging the question.

"I'd better go back. I have to get back to the diner," Kieli said quickly, shaking her arm free.

"Oh, I'll go with you—" Harvey started, turning back to Kieli, but then he broke off and seemed to think for a bit. He looked back again at the woman.

"I'm going to take her back to work. Wait here an hour."

"An hour? Honestly... any girl would just go home."

"Then I'll go to your house later. Where do you live again?"

"Um, I can get back on my own," Kieli interrupted, her head spinning in confusion at their strangely friendly exchange. "I came on the bike, and you'd fall off, Harvey, so I should just go by myself."

She insisted, leaving no room for argument, and turned

around. She ran up the steps, left the hall, straddled her bike, and ran away as fast as she could, without looking back.

*Ran away.*

When the words floated into her head, she wondered why she had run. She didn't really have any reason to.

"You're not very smart, are you?" After she pressed him about Kieli, he had no choice but to tell her the whole story—no, he left out quite a lot, but he told her—to an extent—the whole story, and that was the first thing she said.

"Things might be fine now, but what are you going to do later? She's not like you; time passes normally for her. She'll catch up to your age and pass it before long. Are you going to abandon her when that happens? Or can you seriously mean to take care of her for her whole life? Are you prepared to be responsible for that girl's life? Are you sure you *can*? Even if you do take her everywhere with you until she dies, what'll you do after that?"

"Oh, shut up. It's too late to tell me all that *now*. I'm thinking about it," Harvey retorted, fed up with her tirade.

The woman before him pulled out what seemed like her umpteenth cigarette from Harvey's pack with her lips (*She keeps helping herself. These are mine. Why doesn't she ever smoke her own cigarettes when I see her?*) and answered, "So you are *thinking* about it, but you're putting off coming to any conclusion."

"......"

She made the statement so definitively that Harvey couldn't

argue, and he fell silent. He pulled out a new cigarette of his own to hide his discomfort. When he picked up his lighter, the woman took advantage and brought the tip of her cigarette close. (*Use your own, damn it!*)

Apparently someone was winning big at a table somewhere, as muffled applause rose through the hall from the other side of the purple smoke, but neither of them showed any particular interest. They continued their whispered conversation, bringing their faces close above the small, round table, so that their very existences blended into the tumult around them.

"Why did you hide that girl from me until now? She has something to do with the man you're looking for, doesn't she?"

"Because I knew you would be annoying about her." She had just said exactly what he'd known she would.

"What's the big idea, asking people for favors but not giving them all the information?" Her blue eyes narrowed, a dangerous light inside them. She lowered her voice a notch and Harvey, actually sensing murderous intent in it, pulled back a little.

"...Look, I'm sorry I didn't tell you. And? You found something, right?"

"Yeah, well. I got to talk to someone who has connections to the capital last night, and I made a little progress. It's true that they caught an Undying twelve years ago and brought him to the capital."

"Caught him? So he's still alive!?"

In his excitement, he started out of his chair and almost bumped noses with the woman. She calmly returned his gaze at point-blank range and, after a pause, went on.

"He was alive when they caught him, but it's very possible that he died after that. And that woman who was with him—

from what you just told me, she's that girl's mother? I still don't know who she is. I'll look into it more closely."

"…Okay. Thanks."

He sat back down in his chair, inwardly a little disappointed.

"Oh, I don't mind. But it's not every day you act with some definite goal in mind. Here you come to visit when I've forgotten all about you, and then you want me to help you investigate something. What kind of a whim brought this about?"

"It's not a whim. That's rude. I owe Jude."

One of the reasons Harvey had come to this city was to get information on Jude. He'd thought about passing right through South-hairo and going all the way up near the capital, but then he remembered knowing someone he wished he could forget from this area and decided to stop here first. He kept moving, checking in small towns along the way, then judged this city as most likely, and sure enough, he found her—it was easier to blend in with people in large cities, and thus easier to stay in them longer.

"And I wanted to find out about Kieli's parents for her." That was his other reason.

"…Hey, Ephraim."

The woman's attitude suddenly changed. A slender line of smoke mixed with her sigh, then she went on in a warning tone.

"I'm serious. You should leave that girl with someone before you get too attached. Either way, she's still a normal human being. Someday this situation will go beyond what you can fix. You may look indifferent, but you get emotional about weird things. You can't take a hit, and you take forever to recover."

"Hey, watch it. What's your problem?" Damn woman, listing off point by point everything he himself was already pretty much aware of.

"I'm worried. Frankly, I don't care about that girl. I'm worried about you."

"I don't need you to worry about me, thanks."

"Sometimes you get attached to the dullest things. But you know you're just going to lose them someday, so you make it a point not to think ahead."

"Shut up. Like you have a right to talk, Bea."

"It's Beatrix. Call me that one more time, and I'm done with you forever."

"If you never want to see me again, fine."

"Oh, I get it. I'm helping you this time because I owe you from before, but don't ever come to me with your problems again."

"Same to you."

They both fell into a bad mood, and the conversation stopped short. They smoked in silence for a while.

Not listening to the tumult from the tables around them, Harvey rolled his lighter around in his hands, lighting it and putting it out. "You never fixed that habit. You always do that when something makes you nervous," the woman murmured.

He didn't answer, only looked down and stared at the flame. Maybe the lighter had run out of oil. The flame gradually grew smaller and paler, and eventually went out.

"I-I'm sorry."

It was Thursday evening, and Kieli had just messed up for the third time that day. Counting all the minor mistakes, there were far more than three, but as for the big ones, she'd over-turned bowls of stew twice that afternoon, and just now, she'd hit the cup of coffee she was trying to carry with her fingers and knocked it over.

As she hurriedly wiped up the counter, Buzz called out from the kitchen with a sullen look on his face, "You can just go home."

"... All right. I'm sorry."

She felt dejected and thought, as she got ready to leave, that he might not just mean she could go home for the day, but that she should never come again. She had only one bag to pack. It wasn't just work that had gone wrong: she'd spaced out as she left that morning and forgotten to bring the radio—a big mistake she would normally never have thought possible. The Corporal was probably sulking in the apartment right now.

Even she couldn't figure out why she was in such a quagmire. She might just be hanging on to a weird misunderstanding, and if she asked about it, it might be nothing at all, but, well, Harvey hadn't come home last night. This was a bigger problem than just asking about the circumstances.

She felt strangely relaxed as she thought hopeless things like, "If Harvey never comes back, and I lose my job, I'll end up wandering the streets. How will the Corporal and I make a living together?"

"Kieli."

"Yes, ma'am. Am I fired?" she answered automatically, continuing along her line of thinking, and turned around.

Suzie blinked. "What are you talking about? You don't seem to be feeling well, so when you get home, I want you to stay warm and go to bed. You don't have a fever, do you?"

Kieli gaped for a minute. She didn't expect such consideration.

"...Oh. I'm fine. Thank you."

She bowed politely, a little at a loss.

She went outside through the door on the side of the kitchen. She looked up at the sky through the gap in the alley. It was the orange color of twilight, and the smoke spewing from the diner's exhaust pipe turned the same color and melted into the sky.

When she turned out of the alley and onto the surface street, someone suddenly called out to her. "Yoo-hoo! Hello!" She stopped and looked around, then caught sight of a three-wheeled bike parked across from the diner.

Its driver was resting her arms on the handlebars and grinning in Kieli's direction with her chin in her hands. Her tidy appearance was different than it had been the night before, and her long blond hair, fluttering in the wind, was all tied back. Nevertheless, she was very attractive, whether she dressed up or not.

"Hello..." Kieli answered halfheartedly, then pulled herself together and went toward the woman. "Are you sure you were okay the other day? I think I might have really hit you." She chose to talk about when they first met rather than the previous night.

"Yes. Actually, you did hit me," came the ready answer. Kieli just stood there at a loss for words. The woman indicated her arm and thigh and said, very calmly given the subject, "I had cracks here and here, and there was an incredible bruise. It wasn't funny.

"You see, I'm just like Ephraim."

"...Huh?"

Kieli couldn't quite grasp the meaning of those words right

away. The woman's blue eyes, so much like Becca's eyes, smiled mischievously, so much like Becca's smile.

"We can keep walking, but can I talk to you for a bit? I need to see Ephraim, so I was heading to your place anyway."

To kill time, Harvey went all the way to the Church's branch office and took a look at the face of this "adviser to the parish's chief priest." He was a slim man wearing black robes—he resembled Joachim, which repulsed Harvey immensely. It was probably the fact that he was somewhat like Joachim that remembering that idiot's face repulsed him so much.

*Now I'm even more depressed....*

He had been having the worst time, in several ways, since the night before. Even he couldn't figure out why he was in such an emotional swamp.

He had meant to kill time until morning, but he killed too much of it. By the time he got home, the afternoon had passed, and it was evening. He was understandably tired, and he practically leaned on the door as he opened it and went inside. He would just lie around on the sofa until Kieli got back (though that's what he always did). And then he would probably have to tell her about last night.

"Wah!"

As Harvey walked through the dining room door, he felt a murderous aura and instinctively twisted around. A mass of air, like a sharp blade, flew by, grazing his side, and crashed into the front door. It didn't break through, but a part of the iron door caved in with a spectacular bang.

"Wha...!?" he started to say, but the word died in his mouth. He just stared in shock at the mangled door with his jaw hanging open.

Finally, he found his voice again. "What are you thinking!? We're *renting* this place!" he yelled, turning back toward the room. He couldn't believe what had just happened—of course there was the door, but if he hadn't dodged, he wouldn't have gotten out of it unharmed, either.

*"You don't just stay out until morning—you're out all day, too. Aren't you all high and mighty...."* he heard a low, strangled voice rasp from the sofa under the window. The last rays of the setting sun created a dull spot of light, and the rusty radio sat alone in the middle of the sofa underneath it. Black static drifted around it, like a shapeless mass of microbes.

"What are you gonna do about the door, damn it?"

*"What have you been doing?"* came back the question, completely ignoring Harvey's.

"...Nothing worth talking about. I played some cards, then I wandered around thinking about stuff," he paraphrased, leaning his shoulder lightly on the door frame. To be honest, it was partially that he didn't want to see Kieli's face too soon. He got the feeling that he would have to come to some kind of conclusion about that problem when he did.

*"Did it even occur to you that Kieli would stay up all night waiting for you to come back?"*

"......" Ah, come to think of it, that *hadn't* occurred to him.

*"Do you remember what I told you before? I thought I told you to think more like Kieli. You're not sorry at all that you forgot about her birthday, are you?"*

"Why are you bringing that up again now? That was days

ago. Let it go," Harvey spat out recklessly. He really didn't know what it was, but he was tired today. It was too much trouble to even talk anymore, but it didn't look as though the radio was going to let him go.

"*Of course I'm bringing that up now! That's where you're lacking in sincerity!*" it shouted angrily.

"Sincerity?" What the hell? He was sick of having such abstract things demanded of him as if they were so obviously simple, and at the same time, it made him strangely angry, so an argument rose from him unbidden: "What, you want me to apologize?"

"*That's not the prob—*"

"If being sincere will turn back time to her birthday, then I'll apologize as much as you want. If it could turn back time to the War, I would get on my hands and knees and beg forgiveness. I would do it as many times as I have to if it would make it so I never killed you. If sincerity would cancel out all the murders I've committed—"

"*That's not what I'm talking about!*" Harvey felt as if he would have gone on forever if no one stopped him, but the radio's angry shout interrupted him. "*I'm just telling you not to betray Kieli's trust!*"

"And that's a pain in the ass! There's no guarantee I won't betray her, so it's easier on me if she doesn't trust me! It's just a burden, to be honest!"

Harvey shouted more loudly than he had planned, and he regretted it immediately afterward as a blast of air flew at him.

He brought his arms up out of reflex and blocked the shock wave, but it sent him flying backward, and he crashed into the door. A thud rang out, duller than before, but heavier. Or maybe he had heard it inside his body.

"Hey! I told you, we're *renting*...." He coughed, peeling his back from the dent it made in the door and somehow managing to stand up. That was an effective hit. If he hadn't blocked off the pain at the last minute, he would have been in serious trouble. He staggered to the wall and looked at the left arm he was leaning against. Half of the flesh had been sliced off from the back of his hand to the elbow, and he could see a little bone. The metal frame of his right arm was warped slightly as well.

"Damn it, just because I can take it doesn't mean you should dish out as much as you want...."

He thought he heard something snap inside his head.

In the dining room, growing dark in the setting sun, greenish black static swirled in the air above the radio. The static gathered, gradually forming a blurry, human silhouette: a one-legged soldier, wearing a brimmed hat low over his eyes. "Oho...? You haven't made an appearance in a while...." A smirk rose unconsciously to Harvey's lips.

"*Why you...*" When the static soldier opened his mouth, a low, groaning voice sounded from the radio's speaker. The ceiling light that hadn't even been on crackled and flickered, and the chair and sofa in the dining area started to shake, making noise against the floor.

"*Try saying that to Kieli. I'll kill you.*"

"Go ahead and try."

They exchanged fighting words—the next instant, the static soldier's mouth burst open, and the speaker howled, releasing a wave of high, earsplitting noise.

Harvey twisted out of the way and barely managed to dodge;

the shock wave grazed his cheek and flew behind him, this time destroying the door. He confirmed that fact just from the crashing sound behind him as he raced down the hall and dove into the inner room. Just then, a dining chair danced into the air and charged at him, as if an invisible hand had thrown it. He didn't have time to dodge, so he blocked it with his right arm. In that second, the next shock wave attacked him, and he couldn't defend himself. It landed directly in his side.

But by that time, he was sliding baseball-style into the sofa and giving the radio's speaker a sharp jab with the elbow of his prosthetic right arm. The round speaker caved in with a *crack*.

"*Da—!*" Looking as if it was about to shout one last thing, the image of the soldier wavered and flickered out. The dispersed black static melted into the air a little later.

Harvey figured that it all took about three, four seconds at most.

After that, he lay still with his upper body facedown on the sofa for about ten times that long.

"...Serves—" he finally rasped, with a sigh. "Serves you right. You won't get me every time," was all he muttered, then he lay there limp for an even longer time, lacking the will or the energy to get up. In a corner of his eye, he noticed the blood dripping from his side and forming a black pool under the sofa, and his anger flared up again.

*Who's Ephraim?*

Kieli muttered the phrase over and over in her mind as she walked beside the woman, hanging her head.

She didn't think she would ever be able to like this woman who called Harvey by a name from a past Kieli didn't know. She did know that was Harvey's other name. But to Kieli, Harvey had been Harvey ever since she heard his name for the first time at Easterbury Station, and he was never once somebody called "Ephraim."

The woman said she was just like Harvey, so Kieli guessed that meant that she had been alive since the War—she had never imagined there were women Undying, but there was no reason to think it strange that there had been.

"So you're an orphan? The way I heard it, you resisted the Church, got chased out of your orphanage, and now Ephraim's taking care of you?"

"It wasn't an orphanage, it was a boarding school," Kieli corrected her in a stiff tone, fixing her gaze on the asphalt diagonally below her. The other parts seemed kind of wrong, too, but the meaning came across well enough, so she decided not to care.

Kieli didn't really adjust her pace as she climbed the slope to her apartment, and the woman walked beside her, pushing her three-wheeled bike and wearing a cool expression. But three-wheeled bikes, with their giant fossil fuel tanks, weren't supposed to be light enough that a woman could push them so easily.

"So how long are you planning to tag along with *Ephraim*?" she asked frankly, and, in a sense, quite rudely.

"I plan on tagging along as long as *Harvey* doesn't tell me not to," Kieli answered, speaking quickly and still looking down.

The woman closed her mouth for a time, so Kieli shut her lips as well, and they walked side by side up the slope in silence for a while. The last rays of the sun disappeared in the shadows of the buildings' roofs, and the brief, orange-colored twilight came to an end as the long, blue-gray night fell. As if matching their pace to gradually show them the way, streetlamps lit up, one by one.

"You know that Undying are immortal and don't age, right?" The woman resumed her questioning. Kieli furrowed her brow a little and looked sideways at her.

Even if she hadn't met Harvey, everybody knew that. They were "moving corpses," with eternally operating power sources instead of hearts. Made from the recycled dead bodies of soldiers in the old War, they were said to have gone on killing sprees across the planet.

Why would she ask something so nasty? Kieli had thought she was a nice person when they'd first met, but now she was positive that had been a mistake. In her mind, she resolutely withdrew her first impression that this woman resembled Becca. Becca was mischievous and selfish and spoiled, but she would never be so insinuating and mean.

She didn't answer out loud, only nodded sulkily in the affirmative. "Oh, good. You do know," the woman said, smiling with relief. Was she making fun of Kieli just now? "And you're not like that. You're a normal girl, you know?"

"... What are you trying to say?" Kieli asked in return, in a low voice clearly revealing her suspicious attitude.

The woman turned her gaze forward again and continued. "I hear it was your birthday the other day. Happy birthday."

Her congratulations lacked sincerity, and Kieli answered, "Thanks," with a scowl. So Harvey had told the woman that much. It wasn't really a problem for her or anything, but she had never even imagined him talking about such everyday things with anyone other than herself.

Still facing front, the woman glanced over at her, then looked ahead again.

"Maybe you were just happy and didn't mean anything by it. But you probably didn't consider what he was thinking then. *You* might grow up, but he won't get any older. Have you ever thought about how it feels to be left behind?"

Three steps.

Kieli walked on, then stopped.

She turned haltingly back toward the woman. The woman, too, had stopped pushing the bike, and she coldly caught Kieli's gaze as she looked up at her. Her clear blue eyes seemed to have sunken to a dark color under the night sky.

"You're the only one who was happy. It's selfish of you to ask him to celebrate with you, and not only is it annoying to him, you might as well be deliberately tormenting him."

"That's…not true…," she tried to counter, but her voice caught in her throat and the sentence disappeared, unfinished.

Now that it came up, it was true that Kieli had thought only about herself that day. It never occurred to her what a birthday might mean to Harvey, but…but…. She tried to argue in her head as she thought back on it. He did apologize for being late, and he did eat the cake with her, but more than anything, she didn't want this person she didn't know suddenly being the one to point this stuff out.

"If you really care about him, I'm saying this for your own good: Just get away from him as fast as you can. That's what I wanted to tell you. The longer you put it off, the more painful it will be, for you, too."

"That's—" Kieli interrupted, suddenly facing forward. "That's not your place to say." She said it over her shoulder as she started to walk again, so quickly she was almost sprinting. She passed by the apartment and turned onto the outside stairway beside it.

The woman followed behind her, pushing her bike. "If it's not *my* place to say," she pursued, "then you'll agree if I get Ephraim to tell you, right?"

"Harvey wouldn't..." Kieli started to object automatically, then her feet stilled to a halt again.

She glared at the first step on the flight of stairs ahead of her and bit her lower lip. In a corner of her heart, she was always worried that he might say something like that someday. Or that he might disappear one morning without a word.

The woman glanced her way as she stopped her bike beside the stairs and deliberately sighed.

"Well, I don't think he'll say it, but that's just because he's not thinking too hard about the future. He's always had an unconscious habit of avoiding thinking about anything that bothers him."

"Wh-what do *you* know...?"

"I at least know more than you."

"Because you're an Undying, too? I...I wish I was like Harvey, too, you know!" she wailed unthinkingly and glared up; that instant, the woman's palm flew at her. Kieli gulped, forgetting even to close her eyes. The hand stopped right before slapping her face, and Kieli's bangs fluttered a little in the wind it had created.

"...You're the one who doesn't know anything," the low, quiet voice came from above her. They were a completely different color, but for some reason, in the blue eyes, purposely devoid of emotion, she saw Harvey's.

"It's not your place to yell at me, either!" Kieli managed to squeeze that one line out of her throat, suppressing the trembling in her voice, then spun around and escaped into the stairway.

Her trotting footsteps rang from the galvanized metal stairs as she made excuses in her mind: *I didn't mean to say that. She just provoked me.* But she didn't think it was fair. Kieli was sure that that woman had known him much longer than she had, and her circumstances were more similar to Harvey's, so of course she would know Harvey better.

*I know I can't be with him forever.*

It really stung somehow, and her eyes filled with tears. Was it wrong to want to be with him a little longer despite all that? Why should she have to listen to this woman who appeared out of nowhere and talked as if she was trying to destroy the time they had now?

She ran to the third floor in one sprint, stepped out into the hall, and stopped for a minute, panting. She threw her gaze pleadingly at the second door down: their apartment, where Kieli, Harvey, and the Corporal all lived together.

A foolish, confused sound escaped her mouth. It sounded more like an "Uh?" than any real word.

There was no door in the doorway. But there was a spectacularly deformed rectangular iron plank lying outside it.... She heard the *click* of a door opening and looked up to see the resident of the apartment one door past theirs peek out a little and then immediately rush back inside, afraid.

"Wh-what...?" She gasped and ran through the door—or rather, the empty hole—and through the hall, then stopped in front of the entrance to the dining area.

Faint bluish light from outside illuminated the sofa under the window of the gloomy room. Kieli saw the terrible scene spread out before her and froze in shock. The dining table was lying on its side, and the legs and seats of the two chairs that used to be there lay in pieces across the floor. Small, sparkling bits were scattered everywhere. They were pieces of the light from the ceiling.

"Harvey...! Corporal?"

She peered into the bedroom and naturally saw no sign of Harvey, but there was no hint of the radio, either. She remembered forgetting it and leaving it on the sofa that morning, then hurried back to the dining area and started toward the sofa; but after one step, something caught her eye. She stopped with a gulp.

Under the sofa, which was tilting on its broken leg, there was what appeared to be a pool of black water.

She figured it was blood.

Before she thought about anything, she turned around and dashed out of the room. "What's going on!?" At the doorway, she crashed into the woman, who had come up the stairs behind her.

"Out of the way; this is serious!" Kieli shoved her away and ran into the hall, trampling on the iron board and tripping over her feet toward the stairs.

"Wah!"

At the corner of the hall, her head rammed into the chest of someone who had just come up the stairs. Without even looking, she knew who it was from the smell of tobacco on his shirt. She grabbed at his chest and clung to him.

"Harvey! I think we've been robbed! The Corporal...!" She

looked up, pleading desperately, but he didn't seem particularly surprised as he looked down at her with his usual unemotional copper eyes.

"Robbed?" he muttered, then glanced at the twisted metal plank—the remains of their door—lying in the hall and, with a look of almost admiration, said, "Oh, if there was a thief that'd go that far, I'd actually like to tell him he was kind of refreshing."

"Harvey...?"

She got a contradictory impression, as if he was the same, but somehow different; and Kieli automatically backed away a little. That's when she noticed that Harvey's left arm and left side were covered in blood. She remembered the pool of blood under the sofa.

"What's wrong? What—"

"It's nothing. We just had a little fight is all."

"Little...?" The room was in shambles, the door was gone, Harvey was covered in blood, and he called it "little"? Kieli looked up in mute amazement as Harvey furrowed his brow in annoyance, maybe irritated that he had to explain.

"The Corporal! Where's the Corporal?"

"I threw him away." He practically spat the answer.

She couldn't understand what he meant. She opened her mouth two, three times, then, "Threw him away...?" She was about to question him when Harvey suddenly seemed to notice something and shifted his gaze to the doorway. He made a face of the utmost irritation.

"...Bea."

"Beatrix." The blond woman appeared in the doorway, her clear voice ringing out over Harvey's murmur.

"Don't come in here. What do you want?"

"What a thing to say. I wish you'd at least thank me for all the trouble you put me through."

Their threatening glares and conversation collided above Kieli's head. The atmosphere was tense, very unlike the previous night.

"Looks like you've really done a number here. You were never able to live a normal life anyway."

"I doubt you came here to make sarcastic comments."

"I don't have that much free time. Did you think about what I said last night?"

In response to her question, Harvey clicked his tongue and turned on his heels without a word. He was about to go back down the stairs he had just climbed. "Harvey, wait!" Kieli hurried a few steps below him and stood in his way.

"Hey, what do you mean you threw him away? You and the Corporal had a fight? Why?"

"I'll tell you later."

"Why can't you tell me now? Is there something you need to do?"

"I can't go out without something I need to do?"

"Well, you're hurt, and you just got back. You didn't come home last night, either."

Harvey tried to push her out of the way and get past her, but she clung to his arm.

"Don't run away. Tell me why, Harvey!"

"No one's running away. Move."

He shook her hand off roughly, and it flailed in the air. She stumbled and staggered backward. Her heel missed the step and she dropped down. "Ah...!" someone cried out in shock—

she felt as though it wasn't her voice, but Harvey's. Or maybe it was both.

The scenery spun before her and she saw the night sky overhead. She didn't know how far down she fell, but it felt like only a second later that she heard the *wham* of an impact somewhere in her head just before her vision went completely gray.

A little later, red started seeping in from the edges and colored everything.

He thought the world had gone black and white.

A gray stairway, a black-haired girl fallen on the landing, her white profile and closed eyelids. Gray, black, and white; those were the only colors he saw as he froze, staring at the scene below him. Eventually, a red stain spread from the girl's temple, invading his monochrome world with the bright color of blood.

The image entered Harvey's vision, but he couldn't think about what it meant. Stairs, a landing, a girl, fallen, a pool of blood, stairs, a girl—what was this? It made him sick.

"What are you doing? Out of the way!"

Someone suddenly shoved him aside. He staggered and leaned on the handrail. A woman with long blond hair rushed past him and ran down the stairs. She crouched down in front of the girl, quickly assessed the situation, then shot her gaze up at him.

"Stop standing there and help me, Ephraim!"

Hearing his name freed him from his paralysis.

He practically fell down the stairs and knelt by the girl. "Kieli...." He touched her temple with his fingers and involuntarily pulled them away at the feel of the lukewarm blood—his left hand was beat up and covered in blood, too. He couldn't remember why.

He reached out again and timidly touched the girl's face.
"Kieli, hey...?"

He called her name, but the girl's eyes stayed firmly shut and she didn't move. She didn't move...why not? Because she fell down the stairs. Because someone pushed her. Who...?

*Me?*

"Oh, I'm so ashamed. One of our lovers' spats got a little out of hand. I hope you'll pretend you didn't see anything."

As she said it, even Beatrix couldn't imagine just how epic a lovers' quarrel would have to be to bend a door and knock it off its hinges. As the doctor cocked his head suspiciously, though, she used her best professional smile to flatter him and drive him off. She thought she would hear someone chime in from behind, asking who was having a lovers' quarrel with whom. When nothing came, she was a little disappointed.

*I'm not putting on this ridiculous show because I want to, you know....*

No one was asking, but she made the excuse inwardly anyway as she did what she could to force the mangled door back into place (though it was covered with holes) and went back inside the apartment.

She looked at the dining room, still in shambles, and gave a light sigh, then peered through the bedroom door.

"He says there's nothing to worry about. The cut wasn't as deep as we thought, and she'll be fine as long as she wakes up. Honestly, you people are so much trouble." Acting like such a nice person gave her the creeps, if she did say so, so she added some criticism at the end.

She waited a little, but there was no response from the bedroom.

In the dim light, a girl slept in the bed inside the room, gauze over the right side of her forehead. A young man with copper-colored hair sat next to her, not in a chair, but on the floor, leaning against the edge of the bed. He didn't watch over the girl, but rather turned his back on her, and when Beatrix checked what he was doing, it was just a meaningless cycle of rolling his lighter in his hands, then lighting it and staring at it.

She'd forced him to change his blood-covered clothing before the doctor arrived, but she could still see his wound from the sleeve of his left hand, the one holding the lighter.

Beatrix sighed and leaned lightly on the bedroom doorway.

"To be honest, I'm surprised to see that you're so attached to the girl that you can get *that* hopeless. What's so special about her?"

No reaction.

"This turned out not to be serious, so that's fine. Still, I know that someday, something will happen that you won't be able to fix. You're a fugitive yourself. You can't live a life free of danger."

No reaction.

"And besides, that girl is too heavy a burden for you. An immature, inconsiderate brat like you who can only move at his own pace—there's no way you could keep taking care of someone else. That girl's life won't last long. If you keep dragging her around with you everywhere, you'll completely ruin it. Are you prepared for that? Are you confident that you won't regret it?"

No reaction.

"Hey, there's still time to turn back. You should leave that girl with someone, do something, anything to give her a normal life back. That would be better for you and for her."

No reac—

But this time, he did react. Without warning, he got up, shoved his hands—lighter and all—in his pockets, and walked toward her. He was about to keep going and leave without a word, so she asked, "Where are you going?"

"I'm going to get the radio," he murmured in a whisper, not looking at her as he passed by.

"Look, I'm trying to have a serious conversation here. You could at least listen a little!"

"I was listening."

"......" His response was so unexpectedly frank that she couldn't voice her next complaint right away.

After he left the bedroom, he stopped once. "I'll give it a little thought. Real thought," he said without turning around, then left the hall without further hesitation.

Beatrix stood gaping, listening to the thud of the door falling into the outside hall. It surprised her. She didn't think he would actually listen. She may have been the one trying to persuade him, but she actually hadn't expected much.

"Huh? It's gone...," he muttered to himself as he kicked through the mountain of trash.

The corner in the alley behind the apartment building had an area that had become the neighborhood trash heap. It was doubtful that anyone came to collect it, though, and the trash accumulated in large mounds. He searched for a while, relying on the light from the streetlamp some way off, but the piece of junk he was looking for was not where he thought he had left it.

*Maybe it walked back on its own?*

Harvey realized how stupid it sounded the instant he thought it, but a second later, for some reason he started to seriously think that it might have really happened.

He imagined two feet with shoes sprouting from the radio as it strutted down the street with a strangely bold stride. "Haha…" He laughed out loud in spite of himself, still looking down. As it marched down the road, its speaker kept saying something, speaking quickly. It wasn't the Corporal's voice, but several voices blended together, and they became a monotone voice that didn't belong to anyone: *You're lacking in sincerity trust is annoying there's no guarantee I won't betray her if getting on my hands and knees would make it so I never killed you to be honest it's a burden back to the time of the War murderer don't run away—*

The thought cut off.

Still in the same pose, Harvey gazed at his shoes. The wind blew an empty cigarette box from the mountain of trash. It slid, then rolled down the hill with a dry rustle.

"…I have to find him," he murmured, looking aimlessly upward. By that time, that was all he thought about. He had to find the radio and bring it home. The impetus took hold of him like an obsession, but he had nowhere to look. His gaze wandered left and right.

He noticed a muffled commotion coming from the other side of the building. He felt as if he was only starting to hear it, but maybe it had been there the whole time without registering—he shuddered to think that that was just how dull his powers of perception had become.

Several voices flew about. Apparently there was a group of people. He couldn't make out what they were saying, but from their tones, they seemed to be arguing about something.

"......?"

Harvey found himself heading toward them. He walked over the trash littering the ground and out of the alley, then looked across the street from the shadow of the building and saw about ten people together. He noticed that a few of them held long guns in their hands, and he automatically put his guard up and took half a step backward.

In their motley clothing, they looked like no more than ordinary citizens at first glance, but he could tell from the air around them that they must be the Watch, or whatever it was called. The group had surrounded a short man and were demanding something. They seemed to be out for blood.

He recognized the man: an appearance of indeterminate age that looked both old and young, and—what drew the viewer's attention more than anything—a bizarre monocle eating into his left eye.

The man showed no sign of fear of the thugs surrounding him. "You think you can kill them with those guns? You poor things. You don't know how terrifying they can be." Harvey didn't know what they were talking about, but the man was clearly mocking them. One of the watchmen grew angry and grabbed him by the collar. The small man's feet floated into the air as the large watchman pulled him up, and the radio he held dangled in his hand.... *Huh? Radio?*

"Ah!" Harvey accidentally cried out, and the entire group turned his way. He immediately cursed his blunder. He really must have been out of it to make such a rookie mistake. Instinctively he turned to run, then realized that he was just an ordinary bystander, so he could just walk by like normal, but then again, he had to get back the radio that guy was holding—*Hey, why can't I make such a simple decision?*

While he struggled to make up his mind, the man with the monocle, still hanging by his collar, suddenly pointed at him.

"Oh, perfect. You can try it out by shooting him," he said, and there was no doubt that nobody there, especially Harvey himself, could have imagined what would come next. There was no way they could have. Without warning, the little man grabbed the barrel of the watchman's rifle, pointed it at Harvey's face, and pulled the trigger.

A gunshot thundered through the night street. "Wha...!?" Harvey didn't have time to completely dodge, but he avoided a direct hit. The bullet shaved off some of his right cheekbone as it passed by and pierced the concrete wall of the building behind him. Cries of shock close to screams rose among the men of the Watch.

*Crap....*

He immediately hid his face with his arm and turned around. Right before he escaped into the alley, he saw the monocled man get up with surprising speed after having been flung to the ground, slip through the group of watchmen who were standing ready to flee, and run down a different alley.

"Did you find him!?"

"No, he's that way!"

They were probably looking for the monocled man. Harvey avoided the watchmen running around town, shouting angrily to each other, and took back alleys, navigating in the direction the man had escaped.

*What the hell is with that guy...?*

He'd thought the man was weird from the time he met him at the antique shop, but he'd never dreamed the man would do something so crazy. Harvey's first objective was to recover the radio, but it looked as if he would have to question his assailant about some other things as well.

And then he'd give him a good kick.

*This would scar a normal person for life....*

Harvey cursed, wiping the blood from his cheek with the back of his hand as he ran. The left hand he used to wipe the blood still hadn't healed from when the radio got it. He didn't know what the deal was, but this was a thoroughly bad day. Maybe it was finally time to pay off the karmic tab he had accumulated with his daily conduct.

He saw a few members of the Watch at the end of the street. They were patrolling the area with flashlights, ready to kill. Right before a light came his way, he turned ninety degrees and went down a side road—he didn't know why he had to be on the run, too, but he somehow knew intuitively that making contact with those guys would mean trouble.

He stopped midway down the alley and caught his breath.

He was at a clear disadvantage. He had to make sure not to run into the Watch while finding the guy they were looking for before they did. Just as he felt he had reached a bit of an impasse, he heard a whispered "You!" diagonally above him.

Harvey looked up and saw a shadow peering at him from the corner of a building at the exit of a steeply sloping alley. The black luster of the monocle's outline rose out of the bluish dark of the night. He shuddered for an instant but immediately ran toward it, and the second he got out of the alley, he reached for the man's collar.

"You've sure got guts talking to m—"

The instant Harvey grabbed him, a sudden gust of wind blew from beside him, hitting him with a *whap*. Harvey cut himself off and looked at his surroundings, still holding the man.

The pavement broke off there, and a rock cliff dropped almost vertically at his feet, as if the darkness was sucking the road down into it.

Apparently he had reached the outskirts of town. The place where he'd come out of the alley was the cliff face that bordered the city. A tiered, sloping path formed a gentle arch leading down to the streetlights of downtown, or stretching up to the fault that towered blackly behind the city.

During the day, he would be able to look out over the Southhairo wilderness below the cliff, but now, all that lay there was a pitch-black darkness that gave no sense of distance. An occasional gust whirled around his feet. Understandably, he shuddered and backed away ever so slightly from the edge, then faced the man again. Suddenly a hand was thrust into his face.

"Ack! Don't touch me."

Apparently the blood on his cheek fascinated the man, who

tried to touch it. Harvey started and shook him off. As usual, it was impossible to predict this lunatic's actions.

The man scrutinized the blood on his fingers with his monocle.

"Ah, the blood of an Undying. I knew it."

"...Who are you?" Harvey tightened his grip on the man's collar. "Depending on your answer, I might kill you, so if you want to say your final prayers, do that first." He hadn't yet decided what type of answer would result in this man's murder; nevertheless he questioned him menacingly. His captive seemed unperturbed, however, and sniffed at and licked the blood on his fingers. Harvey felt a chill and immediately slapped the man's hand away as the man answered in a tone that implied the matter was none of his concern:

"I used to work at a lab in the capital. A lab with connections to the Church. I saw your kind there."

"You want to tell me all about it, don't you? That's why you brought it up."

"I wouldn't mind. They chased me out. I have no obligation to maintain confidentiality. Will you come to my home?"

The man answered disappointingly readily and turned his monocled gaze up the slope. Harvey followed his gaze up to the top of the tiered path, where the black peak of the fault lay under the night sky. He remembered the antique shop's keeper telling him that the man was a freak who lived in the ruins. Harvey hadn't thought much about it at the time, but around here "ruins" meant...

"Hey, there he is!"

Harvey turned toward the interjecting voice and saw a member of the Watch run up from the other side of the alley carrying a rifle. Maybe the Watch member himself was surprised that he'd found his quarry. He stood frozen for a second before turning to call for help. Then he looked back at them and cried, "So you two were in cahoots!?"

"No!" Harvey yelled back immediately. He wasn't happy with that misunderstanding. The watchman reacted to his voice and directed his attention to Harvey. That instant, an expression of fear shot across his face.

"Ack!"

With a short scream, he pointed his gun in Harvey's direction. Harvey realized it must have been strange to see someone with half his face covered in blood in the dark of night.

As a shot rang out, the watchman cried out in surprise. (*Maybe you didn't mean to fire, but hey, I'm the surprised one here!*) The bullet drilled into the paved stairs at Harvey's feet, and he instinctively pulled his shoe back. His heel reached the edge of the cliff. He lost his balance and staggered backward.

He simultaneously thought, "I'm falling," and "Should I push the monocled guy away?" and in that instant, he toppled over the cliff, still holding the man's collar.

*I have to get up,* Kieli thought in a panic, but she couldn't lift her head.

She wanted to stand right up and say something like, "Ah-ha-ha, I missed my step. Sorry for scaring you like that," but her body was stuck tightly to the ground, as if sewn in place, and she simply couldn't move.

Her field of vision was pitch-black. She couldn't see a thing. But she could sense that Harvey was nearby. The instant she thought so, a dull light rose on the other side of her eyelids, and in the hazy space it created, she could see the back of a copper-colored head. He sat on the floor, looking down and playing with his lighter in his left hand. It was a gesture she had seen from time to time. She remembered he had a habit of doing that when he was losing at cards.

*I have to get up.*

She thought she needed to hurry and get up and put his mind at ease. *See, look? I'm fine. I'm fine, so you don't…*

*So you don't have to look like you're going to cry.*

His gaze was as empty as always as he contemplated his lighter, and he didn't really look at all as if he was going to cry. For some reason, though, the thought came naturally.

# CHAPTER 4
HAUNTED STARSHIP

She was sure she had slept for several years.

She thought about it, her cheek on her pillow, as she gazed at the profile of the woman standing by the window, and that was the conclusion she reached.

Because as she stood there, Becca appeared all grown up, and had become a beautiful woman. Her long, blond hair with its slight wave and her clear, blue eyes remained the same. She had grown taller and taken on a mature aura, but she still had a little bit of her mischievousness left.

*I'm happy for you, Becca. You grew up. I'm so glad.* She felt it with all her heart. She had become a wonderful woman, just as Kieli had imagined.... She also fleetingly thought that it wasn't fair. Kieli herself might not have grown an inch. She had never expected to become a beautiful woman to begin with, but it was possible she hadn't even changed much from the helpless fifteen-year-old girl who couldn't do anything.

Come to think of it, what time was it? If she didn't get up and get ready, she would be late....

"Wah, I overslept!"

Her own voice, and the pain shooting through the side of her head the instant she got up, woke Kieli completely.

"You startled me. What is this? Don't jump out of bed so suddenly like that."

The woman, who had been looking down outside the window, turned around in surprise. Easy for her to say, but jumping out of bed was "suddenly" by definition.

"Bea..." She was sure that's what Harvey had called her.

"It's not your place to call me that. It's 'Beatrix,'" the woman shot back.

She'd just woken up, and already this person was unflinchingly hostile. Sulking, Kieli put her hand to her head. Something clothlike was spread over the right side of her forehead, which throbbed.

It was her bedroom in her apartment that rose to view in the dim light of the room. Her eyes automatically went to the side of the bed. She had the feeling he had been there a moment ago, but the young man with the copper-colored hair was nowhere to be seen.

"Where's Harvey...?"

"*Ephraim* is out."

"Out where...?"

"I don't know," Beatrix answered curtly, then returned her attention to the window. The bluish color of the night reflected in the glass. In Kieli's grogginess a moment earlier, she'd thought she was going to be late, but now that she looked at her bedside clock, she saw the hands indicating the late hour.

"It's still today, isn't it?..."

"There's no day that's not today. Yesterday and tomorrow are today in their own time, too."

Kieli shut her mouth at the rude comeback, but as the woman hadn't denied it, it must still have been today. She realized briefly that Beatrix must have stayed with her this entire time.

Come to think of it, she got the feeling that in the dream she'd just had, she'd panicked about being late, not to her part-time job, but to class at the boarding school. As a ghost, Becca was rather inconstant, so while she would inevitably appear most mornings, she was fickle, and would sometimes wake Kieli up and sometimes not. As a consequence, she was completely unreliable as an alarm clock.

As she watched Beatrix gaze out the window and thought of

Becca again, Kieli noticed that a shade of caution had risen in the woman's face. She surveyed the streets below with a strangely stern determination, almost a glare. Kieli directed her attention that way and made out, though faintly, muffled noises through the window.

"Did something happen?"

"Dunno. But it looks like things are dangerous out there. They've been making noise for a while now," Beatrix answered, still fixing her gaze on the window, then added, almost to herself, "He sure is late for just going to pick something up...."

The second Kieli heard that, she peeled off her blanket and set her feet on the floor. When she tried to stand, she staggered once. There was still a dull pain in her head, and she suppressed it with one hand.

"Hey, what are you doing?"

"I'm going to look for Harvey."

"Don't be stupid. Stay in bed. We don't know that anything happened to Ephraim. Knowing him, he's probably just wandering around somewhere nearby."

"Either way, I have to find Harvey and ask him about the Corporal."

"You can do that after he gets back."

"The Corporal is none of your business. Please leave me alone," she complained stubbornly as she sat on the edge of the bed and pulled her shoes on. This time, she stood firmly on the floor. She retrieved her coat from the top of the blanket and headed for the bedroom door. She realized she was being obstinate; but when the woman said things like "knowing him," as if she was the expert, Kieli couldn't help feeling rankled, even though she knew she shouldn't think like that.

"Look. You may not care, but I don't know what Ephraim will say to *me*," Beatrix's unhappy voice chased after her. Pulling on the sleeves of her coat, Kieli looked back from the doorway.

"He's not Ephraim, he's Harvey. The one I'm with right now—the one who didn't abandon me and brought me with him all the way from Easterbury—is named Harvey; the one living here with me and the Corporal right now is named Harvey, so it's only natural that I would go get Harvey; and if something's happened to Harvey, it's only natural that I would go help him. And you can just stay here and wait for 'Ephraim,'" she said in one breath and left the room.

A boy peered out of a dark window from the second floor of a building along the street. His eyes met Kieli's for a second, and while there was probably no meaning behind it, the boy waved his hand a little. She returned a meaningless wave when a woman who appeared to be his mother picked the boy up from behind and closed the curtain.

She heard angry shouts flying at each other in the distance, reverberating between the blue-gray asphalt and concrete walls. The residents appeared to be holing up inside their homes, afraid of the turbulent commotion echoing through the late-night streets.

*I would feel better if the Corporal was with me....*

As Kieli directed her feet toward the commotion, she felt a little forlorn without the weight of the radio hanging from her neck. Harvey said he had thrown it away, so just in case, she checked the trash heap in the back alley but couldn't find the radio.

Anyway, she got the feeling that if she found Harvey first, the radio would come back, too. She didn't know where they had gone wrong, and things had gotten a little strange, but she was sure they would be able to go back to living together, the three of them, as they had until now.

*It'll be okay,* she assured herself with a nod, then, "Oww..." Her head still hurt a little when she moved it. She pressed at the gauze on her forehead with her right hand.

*I'd better hurry....*

As she tightened her expression and quickened her pace, she heard the sound of an engine approaching from behind. It was the familiar sputtering, clunking noise of a running fossil fuel engine that always sounded broken even when it wasn't.

She stopped and turned around. A single headlight came up behind her, and soon a three-wheeled bike stopped directly beside Kieli. A beautiful woman, with her long golden hair tied behind her back, straddled the driver's seat.

She glared at Kieli with the worst of ill-humored scowls and said in the worst of ill-humored tones, "Get on. We'll look for him together."

"No thank you," Kieli replied with a scowl to match hers, faced forward, and walked off at a quick gait.

"Stubborn little—" Beatrix revved up the engine and followed her, drove a meter past her, and stopped again. "He did kind of trust me to take care of you, so I'd be in trouble if anything happened to you. Don't think of it as being for you or me. Think of it as being for Ephraim, or what was that name? Harvey? This is for him. Are you okay with that?"

Kieli passed a few steps ahead of the bike and stopped.

She dropped her gaze to the asphalt in front of her and stood there for a while, then turned around, walked back, and climbed in the backseat without a word. "Hold on tight so you don't fall." She couldn't see Beatrix's face, but she felt like her voice was a little softer than before. Kieli wrapped her arms around the woman's waist and held tight to her back. The scent of soap wafted by for a moment; she had thought her mother was the only woman who smelled like soap, so this was an unexpected discovery. As Beatrix revved up the engine and the bike sped forward, the smell immediately vanished in the exhaust gas that spewed from the muffler.

They descended the hill path toward the center of town, making enough noise to disturb the neighbors in the after-hours streets. The lamps at the edge of the road slid past her vision, drawing lines of yellow light.

The soft blond hair falling down the back in front of her fluttered in the wind and coiled around her face. Kieli shook her head in annoyance and called over Beatrix's shoulder.

"Um, Beatrix…"

"What? I can't hear you."

"Beatrix!" She raised her voice to be heard over the engine and wind. "What's your relationship with Harv…" But her voiced faded again partway through. Beatrix glanced back once, then slowed down a little.

"You don't have to worry. We've been stuck together for so long, it's too late for there to be anything like *that* between us."

"That's not really how I meant it," Kieli said, but inwardly she did sigh with relief, then felt awkward and changed her question.

"Do you know someone named Jude?"

"Kind of. Those three were famous, after all."

"Three?"

"Jude and Ephraim and that psycho idiot Joachim—oh, but you know him, too, don't you? The three of them are pretty well known for defeating an entire corps of armored foot soldiers in North Westerbury all on their own or something."

"Huh…" Kieli listened with great interest. She would never hear anything like this from Harvey.

"I was sure they were all dead, but I happened to meet Ephraim a while after the War. We would occasionally run into each other, or he would come give me something to do for him, like this time."

"Something to do for him?"

"Ephraim hasn't told you anything? Nothing at all?"

She shook her head in response, then realized that Beatrix wouldn't see it. Apparently the message got through, though, and she sensed Beatrix letting out a sigh. "…Honestly, that man. He should just get over himself and tell you."

"What? Tell me what?" she asked, drawing her face close. Just then—"Ouch!"—Beatrix abruptly hit the brakes, and Kieli's nose ran straight into her back.

"Wh-what?"

"…Oh, no," Beatrix muttered, then suddenly turned the bike around. Kieli had been rubbing her nose with one hand and almost fell off the bike, so she hurried to wrap her arms around the woman again. The second she thought they were off and running, there was another abrupt stop, and she hit her nose again.

"What's going on...?"

She started to get angry and looked up, then gulped and froze at the scene that greeted her over Beatrix's shoulder.

There were shadows at the top of the slope ahead of them. Not just one or two, but five or six people stood blocking the way, and more people came out of the alley to join them. They were men in common civilian clothes, but black cylinders in a few of their hands shone dully, reflecting the streetlights—the rifles of the Watch.

She heard footsteps behind them and turned her head, still holding on to Beatrix. Similar shadows appeared a few at a time from the alley at the bottom of the slope and blocked their path of escape. "How could I let this happen...?" a strangled voice reached her ears.

"Beatrix?" Kieli turned forward and peered over Beatrix's shoulder to see her face.

"It looks like Ephraim wasn't the one in trouble—it was me. It really was a bad idea to talk to that man...."

The woman clicked her tongue and bit her pale red lips hard enough to cut them.

"Beatrice," came a voice from among the watchmen ahead of them. Judging from the demeanor of the troops, the most important man was the large one standing in the middle, but the one who spoke was the one who stuck close to his left.

The speaker shot Kieli a suspicious glare from over Beatrix's shoulder, as if to say, "What's with the girl?" Then the back in front of her shifted to the side a bit, blocking Kieli's view so that she could only guess what was going on ahead from the conversation.

"That's 'Beatrix.' Can't you remember anything? Apparently the alcohol got to your head before it destroyed your liver."

"I don't give a damn about your name now, Beatrice." The man shrugged off Beatrix's insult with a hiccup of a laugh and went on to say, "I know what you really are. You're the female Undying who escaped at the Great Fire of Toulouse."

Kieli rummaged through the depths of her memory and found that reference in a small column from her Church history textbook. Toulouse was a city on the outskirts of Westerbury parish, where they'd once had a "witch hunt" or something. The calamity that had burned the city down when the witch escaped was known as the Great Fire of Toulouse.

"You don't have to brag about it. You're not the one who figured it out anyway." Beatrix sighed. "I was careless to talk to that priest from Westerbury. It's no surprise that a priest from there would recognize my face. Well? Don't tell me you think you can do something to me with your poor excuse for artillery."

Her voice lowered in pitch and echoed dangerously through the darkened streets. There was a moment of silence as the man apparently faltered, then he continued.

"Either way, don't think you can escape. Church Soldiers will be here from the port soon."

"Oh? Then you should have just been good little boys and left it to the Church Soldiers. I suppose you couldn't wait to claim all the glory. Did you want to be publicly acknowledged again? Well, now I have some time to escape. Thank you."

After the deliberate provocation, Kieli heard the men's murderous murmurs and metallic clacking sounds—the sounds of readying guns.

"Beatr—!"

"We're getting out of here. Hold on tight," Beatrix whispered sharply without turning around, then immediately twisted the accelerator and spun the bike 180 degrees. She abruptly sped toward the wall of watchmen blocking their escape. She'd told Kieli to hold on but didn't give her time to react. If she hadn't already had her arms around Beatrix, she would certainly have fallen off. In a panic, Kieli clung tightly to the woman's back.

"If you don't move, I will run over you!" Beatrix shouted ahead of her. A stir ran through the wall of watchmen. Half of them stayed put and cocked their guns, but the other half broke away. The bike charged right for the weakened wall.

She heard gunshots behind them—behind them? Kieli twisted her neck around, and directly under her line of vision, there was a *thunk* as something hit very close to her rear end. Smoke rose from the fuel tank under her seat.

"What are you thinking!? I've got a normal girl here!" Beatrix looked back and shouted. Kieli was already facing forward when she heard the next volley of gunshots—this time from ahead—as the bike's front tire popped and flew away. The two back wheels spun into the air and flung Kieli's body forward.

She screamed.

"Kieli!" Of course the voice she heard and the hand that grabbed her belonged to Beatrix, but for some reason, she thought for a second that Harvey had come for her.

Kieli closed her eyes and clung to Beatrix, so she couldn't

tell for sure, but they probably hit the asphalt and rolled over a few times, stopping when they hit the concrete barrier of the curb.

At the same time, a spectacular crash rang out nearby. Apparently the bike had rammed into a wall.

It took her a while to relax her body after they stopped, and as she held her breath and froze, her face still pressed to Beatrix's chest, a short sound came from Beatrix's mouth, and the arms embracing Kieli loosened their hold. Kieli gasped and jumped back. "Beatrix!"

"You're not hurt, right?" Beatrix asked her before she could speak further, and Kieli spot-checked herself. "I have a lot of scratches," she reported, and Beatrix nodded.

"Good. Sorry, but you're going to have to deal with it."

Beatrix tried to push herself up, then suddenly collapsed into a crouch on the ground. "Damn it...!" She fell onto her side and pressed both hands against her knee, letting out a curse unbecoming of her shapely lips. Her right knee showed under the hem of her disheveled skirt.

Everything below the knee had torn off and was gone.

"No..."

The bike! Her knee had gotten caught in the wheels of the bike as it rolled over with them!

As Kieli started to scream, she heard violent footsteps and sensed several people standing behind them. She swallowed her cry and turned around. Between ten and twenty watchmen surrounded them in a semicircle, about half of them aiming rifles.

One knee on the ground, Kieli moved to cover Beatrix. But a blood-soaked hand immediately grabbed her shoulder from behind, and a voice said, "Out of the way."

"But—!"

"Out of the way," the voice repeated flatly, and Kieli was shoved to the side.

When she stumbled and put her hand on the ground, her fingertips felt skin.

One leg wearing a shoe was lying there.

Kieli automatically pulled her hand away, then gasped and snatched the leg to her chest. In front of her, the bike lay on its side, its back wheels spinning in the air.

When she turned back, she saw Beatrix using the wall to support herself as she tried to stand on just her left leg. As they watched her still try to get up on her own, even after losing a leg, a frightened stir ran through the men of the Watch— maybe one of them got overexcited, because a short gunshot rang out and Beatrix's body snapped slightly backward. Fresh blood poured out and dyed the golden hair on her shoulders.

Low screams came not from the woman who had been shot, but from the men, and there was a metallic sound as they directed their guns at her head.

*No!*

Still clutching the leg, Kieli instantly kicked at the ground and stood up. She ran to the bike handle in front of her and twisted the accelerator with all her might. The back wheels rotated with a groan, and the bike spun across the asphalt, still sideways. It almost dragged Kieli along with it, but even as she almost fell over, she let go of the handlebars in the nick of time.

After that, several things happened in quick succession.

She heard a series of gunshots. The bike spun into the group of men. The men screamed and scattered, and the bike knocked around a few of them who didn't manage to escape. One shot grazed Beatrix's cheek and there was a burst of fresh blood—it was possible Kieli had the order mixed up, but all of the events unfolded around her almost simultaneously.

Unable to process all of the information in her head, she stood in a daze for a second.

Maybe the accelerator grip was broken—the bike kept spinning as its engine ran at full power, and the Watch got farther and farther away. She dashed over to Beatrix, who was trying to pick herself up with her bloody arms, burrowed underneath the woman and lent her a shoulder.

"I don't want your help...."

"If you have the strength to talk, then hold on." And if Kieli had any energy to talk, then she wanted to put that energy into her arms, too. She supported the woman in a pretty unlikely pose and half-dragged her as she escaped into a nearby alley.

She slipped into a narrow alley behind a bar or something, pushed Beatrix into a gap between the liquor bottle cases stacked up in the trash heap, and held her breath as she waited for their pursuers to pass by.

After the angry shouts and footsteps echoing off the concrete walls grew farther away and completely disappeared, Kieli finally breathed a sigh of relief and relaxed her tense body. "I think they're gone...." She sat down against the wall next to Beatrix, exhaled slowly, and caught her breath as she glanced beside her.

Beatrix leaned against the wall, holding her right hand against the left shoulder that had been shot. Like Kieli, she breathed a sigh of temporary relief.

"You can be pretty brutal. Ramming the bike at them…"

Her tone was the same as always, but her voice was rasping, and a grim expression showed on the profile that rose faintly out of the darkness of the alley.

"I was in a daze. I wasn't thinking of anything.…"

"You're really something if you can do that in a daze. I guess I'll rethink my opinion of you."

Kieli blinked and stared at the woman's profile. "Th-thank you." She realized that she'd received a compliment, but as the notion of it actually confused her, she let her gaze escape to her hands.

She was still holding the leg.

"Ack!" She shouted involuntarily and thrust it away.

"Who do you think you are, throwing people's legs like that…?"

"I-I'm sorry."

Beatrix shifted her body with great difficulty and picked up the leg. Then with a, "Now then," to herself, she lifted her skirt up to her thigh and started fitting the severed leg to her knee section, as if she was a do-it-yourselfer making a chair. Kieli couldn't help staring at what was transpiring. Beatrix suddenly stopped and looked up at her.

"…I think you're better off not watching. You'll never be able to eat meat again."

"I-I'm sorry."

Kieli repeated what she had said before, and looked quickly away.

As she had nothing else to occupy her for the moment, she leaned back against the wall and clutched her knees.

She sat in a daze, feeling the cold concrete against her back and the warmth from Beatrix's body lightly touching her shoulder. She didn't mean to think about anything, but various scenes floated into her head of their own accord. Their apartment in shambles; trying to ask Harvey what he meant about throwing away the radio, and falling down the stairs; Beatrix being there when she opened her eyes; going to look for Harvey and being chased by the city Watch; the bike flying; Beatrix's leg...

"...Kh, ngh..."

Before Kieli knew it, tears welled up and overflowed from her eyes, and she was crying uncontrollably. She wiped her tears with her sleeve, still sobbing convulsively. Even her own clothes were dirty with Beatrix's blood. It had already changed from red blood to a blackish stain resembling coal tar. Just like Harvey's, the blood of an Undying.

"Why are you crying *now*...?"

Beside her, Beatrix sighed as if this was too much for her.

"Well, your—your leg, it came off...."

"It's fine. If I stick it back on, it'll connect again soon enough. It would be better if I could stitch it on, but I can't ask for too much right now." As she spoke plainly, she started wrapping strips she had torn from her skirt around the pieces of her leg to hold them in place. "It would be really hard if I lost it completely like Ephraim's arm, but as long as I have all the parts, I can manage. I have to thank you. Your picking it up for me was a big help."

*That's not the problem!* Kieli wanted to wail, but her sobs got in the way. The words didn't form, so she shook her head back and forth again and again. Whether she had the leg or not, Kieli was sure it still hurt. Why did these people talk about such things as if they were nothing?

They sat in silence, and for a short while, Kieli's strangled sobs and the tearing of cloth were the only sounds that resounded faintly against the alley walls.

"…During the War, this happened every day," Beatrix murmured, still gazing down at her work.

"It was especially wretched when two squads with Undying ran into each other. As long as their hearts weren't shot out, they could lose two or three legs and still go at each other forever. Every army kept at least a few *pet* Undyings."

Still convulsing occasionally, Kieli clutched her knees, pressing her cheek against them, and listened to the woman's voice. Her clear, beautiful voice and reserved way of speaking permeated Kieli's hearing comfortably and quietly.

She was a woman, and she was so beautiful. But like Harvey, she, too, must have had some incredible experiences in that bog of a War in the past. Maybe she got covered in wounds and hid in back alleys like they were doing now. What must she have been feeling as she talked so openly about the War that Harvey never wanted to speak of?

"Of course people lost hands and feet, but there were also guys with their innards hanging out, and if they were careless, they'd have no head. They all crawled around the battlefield, looking for the parts they were missing. When that happened, there were people who didn't care if it was theirs or not—they would tear an arm or a leg off of any dead body on the ground and stick it to themselves. During the War, we were convenient tools that never lost their usefulness, but thinking about it rationally after the War, we must have been nothing more than monsters....That's what an Undying is. We're not people you tag along with out of curiosity, or admiration, or sympathy, or feelings like that."

Beatrix finished tying the fabric and raised her face. When she did, the very slightly softer aura from before had vanished, and the same unsympathetic tone from when she first warned Kieli had returned.

"My opinion hasn't changed. Leave Ephraim as fast as you can. If you stay with him, things like what just happened will happen all the time. And when they do, not only will you be completely useless, you'll just be a burden to Ephraim."

"But...!" Kieli started to retort automatically, but she began to get the feeling that nothing she thought would mean much to this woman. She no longer had anything to say. She looked down at the tips of her shoes and thought.

It was vague, but there was one argument she might be able to make.

"Even so..." She spoke slowly, thinking about how to most accurately put it into words. "Even so, I want to be by Harvey's side. Because Harvey made a place for me. Diagonally across from him." She thought of the boxed seats in the train. Ever since they'd started their journey, her place hadn't been beside him or directly across from him, but, she continued, "Diagonally across from him, he made room for me. He didn't open his mouth and say I could be there, but he made room for me...."

"But that was because you selfishly—"

"No, that's not it."

That wasn't what she most wanted to say. She tried to put the words together, but just then, she sensed a commotion approaching on the other side of the concrete wall.

Beatrix took on a stern expression and checked on the street from the shadow of the liquor cases. Kieli, too, cast a glance over the woman's shoulder at the light visible at the end of the alley.

"Looks like they're back. It would be nice if they'd just pass on by...."

"What if they come this way...?"

Beatrix probably couldn't walk very well yet. Kieli had dragged her this far on the strength of blind momentum, but she wasn't confident that she could move very far from here. She bit her lip anxiously, and Beatrix turned her face toward her.

"You've done enough. Go home—" She cut herself off before she finished, then clucked her tongue bitterly. "It's too late for that to solve things for you anymore, isn't it? Honestly, where is that man, and what is he doing? Hurry and pick up your baggage already!"

"Right now, you're the baggage, Beatrix, not me," Kieli retorted, unable to let the woman's remarks pass, and they glared at each other angrily.

*Rustle....*

They heard a sound surprisingly close by. Kieli sensed someone opposite the clamor of the Watch, on the other side of the piles of trash bags—when she turned to look, a giant silhouette stood there, overshadowing the two of them. A terrifying bearded face rose from below the gloom, and Kieli almost screamed but covered her mouth with both hands.

"Kieli," the shadow spoke. His direct tone resembled Harvey's, but his voice was thicker and more powerful.

"I came to find you. Suzie's been worried," he said, and the familiar, giant cook of Buzz & Suzie's Café offered her his large hand.

*We can't trust them. Obviously they're going to sell me over to the Church.* Beatrix struggled, wailing. Kieli frantically tried to calm her down, and Buzz forced her onto his shoulder and labored to carry her through the back entrance of Buzz & Suzie's Café.

Once they brought her into the living room inside the diner, Beatrix finally seemed to accept her plight, and now she clung to a corner of the sofa, curled up in a ball, and played with her tangled, blood-coated hair, a scowl on her face.

It felt like taking in a beautiful but scratched-up stray cat.

As for Kieli, as soon as Suzie saw her, she took notice of the gauze on her forehead and advanced on her threateningly. When Kieli answered with part of the truth, that she had fallen down the stairs, Suzie's energy deserted her, and she sank into a chair.

"Honestly, what in the world is going on?" she said, placing her elbow on the table and resting her head in her hand. She pressed the same spot on her own head where Kieli was injured, a complex expression on her face.

"The Watch was wandering about, so I called around to our regular customers to find out what was happening. They said they were looking for some suspicious people. They said it was a small man with a weird monocle and a young man with red hair. I got worried and sent Buzz to your apartment, but no one was there, and the room had been turned upside down."

"Red hair—you mean Harvey!?" Kieli interrupted. Now it was her turn to press Suzie. "Who was the man with the monocle? Is Harvey with him now? Do you know where they are right now!?"

She practically slammed her hands onto the table, accidentally knocking over the mug that Buzz had just placed there. Coffee with milk in it spilled over the table.

"I-I'm sorry, I did it again...."

It hadn't even been one night since she had been sent home early for making so many blunders. She immediately tried to wipe it up with her sleeve, hating herself. "I got it. Move." Buzz grumpily forced her out of the way, holding a dishcloth.

"Kieli. Have a seat and calm down."

"Yes, ma'am..."

Chastised by Suzie, too, Kieli plopped down into a chair diagonally across from her.

"So you don't know what's going on either?"

Kieli shook her head silently, and Suzie sighed in defeat.

"We don't know where Harvey is either. It looks like the Watch hasn't caught him, but their information is mixed up, too—after a while, the description of the suspects changed. Now they're looking for a woman with long blond hair and—"

She broke off for a moment and glanced back at Beatrix on the sofa. Beatrix, still hanging her head, turned her eyes upward and glared at her for just a second. Suzie muttered,

"Somehow, they're exactly alike" (Kieli thought she knew who Suzie was comparing her to), then turned back to Kieli.

"They say the other one is a girl with short black hair. I just don't know what's what anymore."

"I'm sorry. I hope all of this doesn't cause any trouble for the diner...."

"That's not what I mean, Kieli."

Suzie's tone suddenly turned gentle, and Kieli looked up blankly. Suzie was gazing at her with a soft smile, the smile she often gave to regular customers who came to the shop hungry, an expression that said, "You are hopeless, aren't you?" Buzz, too, had finished wiping the table and was watching over her with his usual grumpy but quiet expression.

"You should have come to us to begin with. You should be more assertive about letting people help you. Because people can't live life without getting help from somebody. So don't be shy, just bother us already. Understand?"

"......"

Kieli continued to gape as she looked from Suzie to Buzz and back again.

"...Yes, ma'am," she said with a small nod after a moment.

And here she'd thought she was relying on them too much already just by getting them to let her work at the diner.... There was something she'd thought occasionally since meeting Suzie and Buzz. Even if this planet is just, and an upright, completely neutral God didn't reach out to people, maybe people like Suzie made the world a little bit kinder to make up for it. If only everyone in the world were like Suzie and Buzz, then this world would be much gentler and more tolerant, and no one would chase after Harvey or Beatrix anymore.

❦

Curled up in a ball on the sofa, it wasn't as if Beatrix had been sleeping, but she found herself half-dreaming, remembering the past.

She remembered that it was a calm morning with no wind. Buried in burned-up rubble, she was gazing absently at the brightening sky. The fire that had burned the city of Toulouse all night long still sputtered in places, and the crackling of flames filled her ears, strangely peaceful. There must have been a burnt corpse nearby because the smell of charred flesh wafted her way, but it wasn't worth the effort to move her head.

She pinched a lock of her burnt, frizzy golden hair and sighed. If she cut it to even it out, it would end up very short. It was short during the entire War. It was a stupid reason, but that was why she liked long hair. She suddenly shifted her gaze from her hair to her hand. It was horribly burnt and blistered. She lifted her other hand, confirming that it was in the same state, and came to the conclusion that the smell of burning flesh came from her, though she didn't much care. The lower half of her body was invisible to her, and it might be in even worse condition. She had no feeling in either of her legs, but of course she didn't care about that either. All she cared about was her hair.

*And I liked it. Such a shame.*

The "witch hunt," the "Great Fire of Toulouse," it didn't matter; the minor historical event that would later be called those things was a story that, in broad terms, was found all the time in old stories and wasn't the slightest bit interesting—they discover that a woman living in town is an Undying; the townspeople capture her and start to burn her at the stake. The fact that an influential person in the city knew she was an Undying and took great care of her anyway, the fact that she had just been starting to believe that if the people of the town would only accept her she could live there forever—there were all kinds of minor facts like that, but to history, they were all insignificant details.

She heard footsteps approaching over the debris. A citizen, or a Church Soldier—she had escaped as far as the outskirts of town, then had run out of the will to try any longer. She lifted her head as if this wasn't any of her concern.

With the sand-colored morning sky as a backdrop, a man with hair the same color as the rusty evening sky stood looking down at her.

"...Ephraim."

She felt as though she hadn't spoken that name in more than ten years. His eyes, the same shade of copper as his hair, stared into her face. Then, after thinking for about ten seconds, he said, "Oh. Is that you, Bea?"

He said it with the amount of emotion she would expect after being apart for a month at most. Was that how he said hello to his old war buddy, who had faced death with him time and time again, when he saw her again after so long? She sighed, thinking to herself that he never changed, and answered with the same degree of disdain.

"That's my line. What are you doing here?"

"There was quite a fire show last night." He nonchalantly surveyed the charred ruins. "It was really burning, so I kept watching. Then it went out, so I came to check it out, and there you are." Apparently it never occurred to him to help extinguish the fire while it was burning. But she didn't really feel like blaming him. She probably would have done the same thing in his position.

"How long are you going to stay buried there? The Church Soldiers'll be here before long."

"I don't care if they catch me. I'm tired." She ignored the hand he offered and averted her face in a huff.

He simply took his hand away and turned on his heel. "Oh, okay. Well, I'm off, then."

"Hey! You came all this way, and you're just gonna leave me?"

"...Make up your mind."

He turned back, exasperated, took her arm, and pulled her out of the rubble. As she held his hand and righted herself, for some reason, she suddenly felt like wailing.

"Listen to this! The bastard abandoned me!" She complained to the skies, still sitting in the wreckage.

He made a face of extreme annoyance. "I don't care. Don't cry to me."

"I'll never trust normal people ever again. Oh, maybe I'll just settle for you."

"I don't think so."

"I wouldn't like it either."

"Then don't say it."

"I regretted it the second I did."

They glared at each other, repulsed with all their hearts. They ran into each other from time to time but never stayed together long, most likely because they both inwardly hated that it always turned into a party of licking each other's wounds.

After a while, he was the one to look away first.

"Can't you walk?"

"I don't know. What do my legs look like?" She hadn't looked at herself yet, so her answer was a little strange.

"...I'm doing you a favor. Make sure to pay me back." He wrapped his arm around her side and easily lifted her up.

"I owe you one." She couldn't work up the energy to resist and obediently put her arm around his neck, gazing at the scenery over his shoulder. A little in the distance, the bell tower of the Church in the central plaza stuck out under the nebulous morning sky. Apparently, the bell tower had managed to avoid destruction, but that plaza was where the fire had started. The area had probably taken the brunt of the damage.

"I wonder if a lot of people died...."

"Probably."

In contrast to the almost unsatisfying peace of the morning, strong winds had blown violently through the town the night before. The bonfire that was meant to burn her at the stake spread and became a giant inferno.

She didn't get angry. She didn't hate them. Even now, there was a part of her that still believed, somewhere in her heart, that she might have been able to live in that town forever—but of course that would be impossible now. She would probably never come back.

"I burned my hair...."

In the corner of her eye, she saw that not only had she burnt her hair, but both of her arms were horribly charred and blistered. Still, in the end, she only murmured about her hair as she watched the smoldering remains of the city grow increasingly distant until she could see them no longer.

*Back then all I thought about was my hair and the town, like an idiot....*

Beatrix heaved a light sigh as she combed her fingers through her blood-encrusted tresses.

Living life as a vagrant for very long, one stopped caring about nearly everything—including oneself—but occasionally one became strangely fixated on the most pointless things, and she wondered why. For her, it was her hair and that town.

*So for him, it's that girl....*

Still resting her cheek on the back of the sofa, she studied the profile of the girl standing in the middle of the room. She thought, "But she's just a normal girl with nothing really special about her," an impression that might offend the girl a little. She watched as the girl changed out of sandals into sneakers and pulled on the stiff goggles for riding three-wheeled bikes around her neck. Then, finally, she started to suspect something.

"Kieli. What are you doing?"

"I'm going to go look for Harvey," Kieli answered, turning to Beatrix and adjusting the band on the goggles. "I got some information. The man with the monocle might be the weird person who lives in the ruins. I'm going to go check it out."

Hearing that, Beatrix remembered that the lady of the house had been making phone calls in another room. Her husband had left, saying he was going to make something for a late-night snack.

"I'm going with you."

"With your leg, it would be hard just riding in the back. You'll just drag me down."

As she sat, unable to respond to the blunt assertion, Kieli finished her preparations and muttered a simple, "All right," as if to gear herself up.

"Hey, wait a second. Going by yourself isn't going to—"

Beatrix hurried to rise from the sofa, but the nerves in her legs didn't work. She almost slid down before she clutched the back of the couch. Kieli turned back from the door and looked at her in exasperation, as if to say, "See? I told you," and Beatrix felt extremely dissatisfied. That little girl was crying just a few minutes ago, so why was she acting as if *Beatrix* was the one who needed looking after?

"Oh, yeah. I didn't get to finish earlier."

"What?" Beatrix asked, her voice unintentionally sulky.

Kieli hung her head a little and dropped her gaze to her sneakers. "Um, I told you before that Harvey made a place for me...," she said, then paused, thinking about which words to use, and raised her face—she didn't look particularly worked up, but wore an expression as if what she was going to say was obvious.

"But the truth is, I think Harvey was looking for a place for himself more than anyone. So I hope I can find a place for him."

As the girl left the room with a "Well, I'm off," Beatrix, unable to come up with anything to detain her, watched the child go without saying a word.

After the girl's footsteps disappeared on the other side of the door, Beatrix leaned against the sofa and sighed. "…That girl is much better prepared for whatever may come," she murmured under her breath and somehow managed to come to terms with something. And she thought, just for a second, that she might be jealous.

Then she looked up at the ceiling and thought:

*That's exactly why, Ephraim. It's because she's so straightforward that she's such an extra burden to an idiot like you.*

"Turn the steering wheel! The steering wheel!"

A wall suddenly filled the round beam cast by the headlights. The second he shouted, the truck took a sharp left, sending up a murderous screech of friction, stopping as the side door grazed the wall a little.

After a pause, there was a *fsshh* behind them.

"I'm tired…."

Forced against the side window that just barely touched the wall, Harvey sighed in exhaustion. A lot had happened, what with having it out with the radio, suddenly getting shot at, and falling off a cliff, but he got the feeling that riding in this truck had put him in the most danger he had been in all day.

Luckily, there had been a rock shelf a few meters below the cliff where he had fallen. Unfortunately, he couldn't see in the night's shadows and ended up hitting his back hard. Still, in the darkness, he was able to wait for the Watch to leave, escape town in the beat-up, three-wheeled truck his companion called his beloved car, and drive recklessly through the dark wilderness, relying on the headlights and the track on the ground. Inwardly, he decided that he would walk home.

"You're a really crappy driver. I'm amazed you've come to and from town so often without dying," Harvey grumbled, narrowing his eyes at the man in the driver's seat.

"If you're going to complain, then you drive. But we're already here," the man answered simply, his tone calm. He opened the driver's-side door and jumped out.

"I suck at driving, too," Harvey muttered, half to himself, then crawled out over his seat and into the driver's. When he stuck his face out the door, the wilderness air brushed his cheeks, carrying a hint of a rusty, metallic scent. He slid from the seat and stood on the ground, savoring the rough earth under his shoes.

It was a world of almost complete darkness. The white light from the headlight was the one thing cutting through the emptiness, illuminating a small, circular area. Sunburnt earth with stones strewn about and a rusty metal wall stood abruptly in the middle of it.

He noticed bent metal pipes poking out of the ground nearby. "Plumbing...you get water?"

"That's how I can live here."

Harvey got closer and tried twisting the faucet. After a burst of liquid and air, muddy water flowed from the tap. "Huh. How long has it been here...?" It may have crashed, but it was still technically a spaceship. This water line had probably been dug by people who had come looking for valuables. Harvey availed himself of the opportunity to stick his head under the faucet and wash the blood from his cheek.

"Is this your first time here?"

"Yeah. My first time this close."

He must have considered checking it out before, so why had he given up on the idea? He couldn't remember the reason, so it must not have been very important. As he ruminated about it, he finished up at the faucet by putting his mouth to it and taking a little drink. It was dirty water with rust and sand in it, but he was used to the taste, so it didn't bother him. Not that he liked it, either.

He shook off the wet hair that stuck to his forehead and made do with wiping his face with the shoulder of his shirt as he looked around. In a corner of the headlights' glow, the man had plastered himself to the wall and was moving something around, pointing his monocle at what seemed like a control panel.

There was a heavy *clunk,* and a rectangular crack sprang into sight a little ways up the wall. A part of the wall floated about ten centimeters up on their side, then slid to the side and formed an opening.

"Huh...," Harvey found himself muttering, without any deep meaning.

The small man had a bit of a hard time climbing to the hatch created in the wall. "It'll close up after a little while," he informed the Undying before disappearing inside. Harvey got closer and peered through. Something like a hall stretched out before him.

"Oof...!" He put both hands on the threshold and kicked lightly off the ground, jumping inside. Just then, *clunk!* The hatch closed, making the same sound as when it had opened.

*He really meant a little while....*

Harvey looked over his shoulder at the wall and shuddered

a little. Thank goodness he hadn't been locked out in the middle of the wilderness.

The cylindrical hall, surrounded by metal walls, sloped steeply upward. As Harvey walked, he wondered why it would turn into a slope, and hit on a very simple reason. He had forgotten because he had seen only part of the outside wall just now, but when he'd looked at the structure from far away, it stuck out of the ground at an angle.

"It still has power...?"

He couldn't imagine how a starship that had crashed hundreds of years ago would still have a working power source, but emergency lights lining the bottom of the wall at equal intervals dimly illuminated his feet. He had muttered it half to himself, but the man walking a little ahead of him answered without turning around.

"I fixed the nuclear reactor in the power sector and remodeled it so it could get a little power from the resources of this planet. But of course I can't create enough energy to get the ship itself to move with the dregs that are left now."

"Huh," he responded, honestly impressed, and hurried to follow the man's back, floating somehow eerily in the dim glow from the emergency lights at their feet. The two sets of mismatched footsteps resounded faintly and indistinctly in the enclosed space as their feet struck the hard floor—he didn't know what it was made of, but the floor, which must have been originally much smoother, was now coarse with layers of dust and fine rubble.

They climbed a good way up the sloping hall to a place where the ceiling and walls had collapsed, blocking the way forward.

His guide went through a crack in the corner and deeper inside.

When Harvey bent down a little and passed through the crack after him, he heard a voice say, "I just got back."

Harvey swallowed and stopped walking. He was appalled at himself. It hadn't even occurred to him to consider the possibility of someone else being there. (He really was in serious trouble today. His ability to deal with danger was completely misfiring. If an enemy had been nearby, he could have shot Harvey right in the face.)

Maybe this was where his host lived. The space was relatively wide, like a division of the ship. Naturally, it tilted at the same angle as the hall, but the rubble had piled up so thickly toward the bottom of the slant that it formed a floor that was relatively flat and stable.

A person's silhouette floated in the center of the room.

The figure wasn't clear in the rough, almost staticky darkness that enveloped it, but it was a woman—or rather, a girl; she was thirteen, fourteen at the oldest. Only her lifeless white face and slender arms rose oddly out of the shadows.

The girl stretched her white hands out to the man and slowly moved her lips.

*Welcome back, Brother....*

A faint, almost inaudible voice sounded in his ears.

"I'm home, Elena," the man answered, standing in front of the girl.

*He can see her...?*

Apparently the guy could see the spirit girl, just like Harvey could. The Undying gaped at the realization, but something felt off.

The girl's face was right in front of the man's eyes, but his unsteady gaze was directed somewhere around her chest. "I know I was out late tonight. I'm sorry you were bored." As he spoke, he still didn't look the girl in the face. The ghost opened her mouth as if she wanted to say something, but he just talked over her—something about how he scared those idiots in town today. Though it was thanks to that scare that Harvey'd got caught up in this mess.

*So he can't see her clearly....*

As Harvey stood in the doorway and surveyed the center of the room suspiciously, his host finally finished recounting all the events in town that day. "Oh, yes. Today I brought an interesting guest." He turned back toward Harvey.

"I don't think I'm strange enough for *you* to think I'm interesting," Harvey retorted with a frown, but the man didn't care.

"First let me fix this. Then we'll talk."

He placed the radio on a worktable overflowing with old computer terminals and scrap metal. (He'd refused to let go of the radio, saying he was going to fix it when he got home.) He pressed the lens of his monocle against the rusty casing and muttered dreamily, "Fascinating. I wonder what kind of spirit is inside."

"...What are you? A paranormal researcher or something?"

There was no way the Church would sponsor a lab for that kind of research, but it was the only thing Harvey could think of, so he asked—the man had claimed to have seen Undyings there. Harvey had followed him out to the middle of nowhere like this so he could press him for more details.

His host answered readily, but so readily his tone was empty, and completely untrustworthy. "Something like that" was his answer.

"'Like that'? So you're not. What was that lab for?" Harvey questioned further. The man had brought his tools to the table and was already repairing the radio. The spirit girl clung to him, leaning on his back. To an outsider, she looked incredibly heavy, but the man just immersed himself in his work, wearing an ecstatic expression that betrayed a hint of madness.

*What is with these people...?*

Harvey sensed an aura of inapproachability about them, and paused so long he ended up missing his chance to continue the conversation. He sighed and shifted his gaze around the room.

He probably got the energy from the power sector he said he had remodeled. He had secured enough light to live by, although it certainly wasn't a brilliant light. As Harvey stood there for a while, looking around, he noticed an iron ladder installed in the wall toward the top of the slanting room—the wall itself tilted, leaning this way, so the ladder went beyond perpendicular and hung at quite an athletic angle.

*There's more above...?*

Harvey casually started walking toward it. Using the metal reinforcements and pipes sticking out of the peeling wall as handholds, he climbed to the top of the slanting floor. As he grabbed the metal frame of the ladder, he heard a voice overhead.

*Huh? There's still someone else...?*

He thought he had heard something, but as soon as he focused his attention on it, it vanished.

Harvey glared suspiciously at the darkness above the ladder, and after a little while, whispered voices leaked through again, like vague static.

*Liberation army…*

*Weapons dealer and sniper…*

He tensed up for a second when he caught the troubling words, but the next things that came to his ears were "Flush," "Two pair," and "You win again?"

Apparently they were playing a game.

He looked down toward the bottom of the room to make sure that the researcher wouldn't be looking up from his worktable for a while, then set his foot on the ladder.

He wasn't faceup, but he was pretty close to it as he climbed the ladder. When he stuck his head through the opening in the ceiling, the first thing he saw was the cloudy, blue-gray sky completely covering the area overhead. The outside night air touched his skin. It was dry air, with a hint of a rusty metallic scent. Sometimes he thought that the smell of the wilderness was the same everywhere on the planet.

He forgot what he was doing for a bit and gazed at the night world extending across his vision, then crawled onto the floor of the deck above him, which tilted sharply, like everything else.

He was at the tip of the starship. It was probably the place they called the flight deck, but all the valuable machinery had been carted off long ago, and an empty space spread before him. A large portion of the ceiling had fallen out, centering around a quarter-sphere-shaped hole that seemed to be where the windshield had been. It had become an observatory from which he could look directly out over the world.

Still, right now, all he could look out over were the shadows of the clouds hanging overhead—but if it had been a night when the twin moons were bright, he probably could have enjoyed the scenery some. The sky was lightening ever so slightly, but it was still too early for dawn.

Harvey was sick of seeing the night sky with nothing in it, but he looked up at it anyway, and as he did, he thought he could see a tiny speck of light beyond the clouds.

"Huh…?" he muttered and blinked once.

When he opened his eyes again, a world of blackness expanded above him, seeming to suck him in.

An ocean of darkness stretched as far as the eye could see. Across its surface twinkled countless particles of light, similar to the city lights he had gazed down on from the top of the hill. Pale blue lights, reddish lights, small, faint lights, bright, cross-shaped lights…Sometimes they would fall, leaving a white tail.

The twin moons, which should only have been vaguely visible through the layers of sand and dust that covered the planet, rose distinctly into the sky. They were spheres with rough, rocky surfaces. It seemed as though gravity could pull them crashing down at any second—

"Wah…"

The illusion caught hold of Harvey, and he cried out in spite of himself. The instant he did, his voice pulled him back to his senses, and his vision suddenly contracted. The next thing he knew, the sky from before—completely buried in low, blue-gray clouds—spread before him again.

Still gazing up, he stood frozen, speechless, for a while.

"Three Moon and Planet Earths."

"Temple flush. Yesss!"

He heard voices behind him. They were the voices from before.

Harvey slowly turned toward them. A dimly lit area rose into view in the middle of the flight deck, like a solitary island suddenly springing to life in the sea of darkness, and several people sat in a circle inside it. One of them, wearing a light blue jumpsuit, seemed especially happy and triumphant at beating the man beside him, who wore the same outfit.

"This time, *I* win."

"It happens occasionally," the other man answered plainly, not particularly upset, and started to nimbly shuffle the gathered cards. As Harvey stood watching them, the first player turned his face toward him.

"Yo. How was the view?" he asked with a carefree smile, playing with his chips in one hand.

He thought for a second, then answered with a wry grin, "...I think it was a little scary."

"You're honest. I like that," the man said and beamed, satisfied.

"Wanna play? The nut down there doesn't seem to notice us enough for us to get through to him. He's no fun."

"Sorry, but I'll pass too," Harvey declined, shaking his head. (It would be hard to play. Their cards were just as transparent as they were.) He did, however, slide down the slanting deck to where they sat.

Aside from the two men in the pale blue jumpsuits, a few others sat in the circle wearing simpler, beige clothes, and they were all enjoying their game of cards. He bent down beside the circle and watched the game, occasionally speaking with the first jumpsuited man.

"You been playing here all this time?"

"Yeah, we've been doing this here for a long time. I guess it's been hundreds of years."

"Even during the War?"

"There was a time when they seemed to be shooting off guns a lot. We've seen some guys like you, young men who don't die. You guys killed a lotta people, didn't you?"

"...Yeah. That's right."

Harvey closed his eyes lightly and nodded. The player broke off the conversation for a time, moving his cards around, a sullen expression on his face, but when he finished, he looked up from his hand and said, "Well, that's war for you. A lot more died in the wars on the mother planet." He laughed cheerfully.

"What was the mother planet like?"

"Hmm, it wasn't much different from this one. It was almost all wilderness and desert."

"Oh."

It wasn't as though he had ever pictured anything in particular, but he'd had a vague idea that it might be prettier. He couldn't help responding with a bit of disappointment, and the second man in the light blue jumpsuit threw some chips into the circle and opened his mouth.

"Do you hate this world?"

"...I don't really like it. But I don't hate it."

Saying the first thing that came to mind, Harvey remembered using the exact same line on someone else. In the recesses of his memory, he tried to remember who it was, and the bright voice of the girl from the fifth floor rang in his ears.

*Do you like this city, mister? I....*

"As for me"—the second jumpsuited man dropped his eyes to his own cards and continued—"I like it pretty well. The land that the prisoners cultivated from a barren wilderness into a place where they can just barely manage to survive, and the new history that was born there." As he said it, he redirected his gaze at the other onlookers around the circle. The men in the beige clothes looked up and smiled, a little bashfully.

"Unfortunately, we can never set foot on this land again. So we want you to ...."

*I really hope you'll like it for me....*

"Sorry, but I can't take your place," Harvey muttered, interrupting him. He had a feeling he knew what he was going to say. "...I'm more like you guys than anything else, anyway." As Harvey said this, he remembered the girl's line. "We're kind of the same, aren't we?" He looked at the circle inside the light and suddenly thought that it might be kind of nice if he could join them, in this place where time stood still, and just enjoy playing cards forever.

"You're not like us," the second jumpsuited man said quietly. "You can still touch the ground with your own feet and walk a path. Your journey must be endlessly long, so maybe you lose sight of the path sometimes. But even so, if you just keep walking, you're sure to end up somewhere."

"......"

For a while, Harvey had no reply.

Still gazing at the man's profile, the Undying turned the sentence over in his mind. "Aw, don't brood about it. He just likes talking fancy, the poet," the first player laughed beside him. His laugh was infectious, and Harvey chuckled a little, too. Wasn't "Don't brood about it" the kind of thing *he* was always telling *her*?

"Well, I guess it's about time to break up the party," the man said as a faint light started to hit his back. He raised his face and looked up outside the flight deck. A sand colored horizon had begun to appear far in the distance of the night world, painted blue-gray.

"Well, you know, if I was to take my colleague's words and paraphrase 'em for you..." As he spoke, gathering up the cards, the crewman's profile gradually grew paler, melting into the morning sun. The beige-clad prisoners went on ahead, disappearing one after another. "You may have a long way ahead of you, but just keep doing the best you can."

"You're paraphrasing too much. That's completely different," his colleague complained, and he lightheartedly replied, "Not that different." Then, bidding Harvey a brief farewell, he said, "Well then. See you again, if fate allows." Then he disappeared with his colleague into the sand-colored morning sun.

*I get the feeling that "fate allowing" me to meet a dead person wouldn't be a very fortunate thing, but....* Because Harvey was thinking of such trivial things upon parting, he missed his chance to say good-bye, and the next thing he knew, he had been left alone on the remains of the flight deck.

*Your journey must be endlessly long....*

Harvey considered again the meaning of the words still echoing in his ears, and still crouching, he looked at his feet. Tattered work boots. He had stopped counting long ago, so he didn't remember how many pairs he had worn out before these.

*Lose sight of it? I've never even seen a path....*

He cursed but then thought it might be because he had never tried to *find* a path. He just wandered aimlessly, carried wherever events took him—come to think of it, what was he wasting time hanging around up here for? Didn't he have something more important to be doing?

*Argh. What, am I running away...?*

He sighed inwardly at his bad habit's reappearance. He'd meant to go out and get some time alone to figure out what he would do next, but he had ended up chasing the still-tangled thoughts out of his head. In fact, perhaps he had even been unconsciously escaping reality, because he hadn't thought once of how Kieli was doing until just this very second. He had taken his frustration out on her, hurt her, and run away.

"I'm so immature...."

He didn't need Beatrix to point it out to him; he was already fed up with his lack of maturity.

Harvey wondered if she was awake yet. Beatrix was probably there with her, but if she woke up and the radio wasn't even there, she would probably feel alone and nervous.

*I guess I'll head back for now....*

He sighed and picked himself up. After he stood, he looked down at the space in front of his shoes one more time, and he really couldn't find anything like a path, but at the moment, he at least knew what he had to do. He had to go home, look her in the face, and apologize.

He could decide what to do next after that.

But Harvey had a feeling that he knew the answer.

As he climbed down the ladder, Harvey twisted his head to see how things were going below, and the monocled man was sitting at his worktable just like before. Maybe he had finished his repairs, because Harvey noticed that he was about to turn on the radio's power. "Whoa, wait a second!" He panicked and jumped off the ladder. The momentum carried him, and he almost slid down the diagonal floor toward the tinkerer.

The man turned around, and Harvey snatched the radio from him in the nick of time. His host pouted like a child who had had a toy taken from him.

"What are you doing?"

"You can't turn him on too suddenly. It'd be *really* bad."

"Why?"

"If you really have to, then do it in the middle of the wilderness or somewhere; anywhere there won't be severe damage." Remembering how things were right before the radio broke—er, before he broke it—Harvey could easily imagine what would happen as soon as the power came on. He knew he had sown the seeds himself, but he still wanted to tear his hair out.

"There's wilderness right outside. No problem," the man said with a straight face, taking Harvey's warning completely at face value. He went on to look, still with a straight face, down at his watch. "Oh, but before that, it's time for breakfast. I promised Elena to always eat breakfast with her. You may join us."

"No thanks. I'm going home," Harvey tossed out carelessly, fed up with the random changes of subject (first of which, he was under no obligation whatsoever to let this man see the radio with its power on), and started walking toward the crack in the wall that they had come in through.

"You don't normally eat? You may not need to eat to keep your strength up, but that doesn't mean you don't get hungry, does it?"

He stopped.

"Your 'core' records all of your cells' information in its memory at the time it starts up, and functions to maintain the same conditions semipermanently, so your cells don't age, and if you get hurt, the wound heals immediately. But other than that, your basic biological activity should work the same as the average human's."

"... My sense of hunger went numb during the War. And I can control my other senses to an extent," Harvey answered in a monotone, but he inwardly raised his caution level to its maximum as he turned around. He had been about to leave without asking this man the most important question.

"Who are you? What kind of lab did you work at?" Harvey demanded, lowering his voice.

"Well, sit. You can at least drink tea, can't you? I promised to always have teatime with Elena once during the day," the man said, his answers not quite meshing with the question as usual, and he put an aluminum pot filled with water over the burner on his worktable (though Harvey didn't think those burners were originally meant for boiling water). He looked over his shoulder at the spirit girl hanging on his back.

"Oh, right. We only have coffee here. I'll go into town again tomorrow and buy your favorite kind of black tea. *Starting tomorrow,* you really will be able to drink tea with me."

The girl wore a dark expression and looked down, shaking her head as if she wanted to say something. It seemed as though the gesture meant she didn't want coffee *or* tea, but the man only nodded to himself, as if agreeing with his own idea, and started mixing coffee powder into his cup.

"You may already be aware, but the magnetic fields created by this planet's fossilized resource strata have the unique characteristic of resonating with spiritual matter. I crafted this monocle from fossil ore. The spiritual matter reacts, and I can see it as wavelengths. Fascinating, isn't it? Would you like to take a look?"

"... No, I'm good." Harvey shook his head, a little repulsed by the man's passionate invitation. If he remembered correctly, the man said he had been chased out, and Harvey could kind of understand why. Becoming so obsessed with paranormal research that wouldn't help or harm the Church, or actually that would *only* harm them, they *would* chase him out. He was lucky they didn't drag him into custody as a heretic.

"So never mind you—what did they do at that lab?"

"The Church gave us money to research pre-War fossil energy."

"Aside from the dregs, there aren't any pre-War energy resources left anywhere on the planet. You can't do research without any material...."

Harvey realized the answer as he spoke, and his voice trailed off.

There was just one kind of resource currently remaining. The final culmination of the advanced energy culture from before the War—he felt his heart pound a little harder.

The liquid inside the aluminum pot started boiling and bubbling. In the midst of their brief silence, the extremely ordinary burbling sounded very out of place. The man didn't look at Harvey, but maybe he sensed the mood around him (or maybe he was just talking because he wanted to—that was a very likely possibility) and nodded, continuing.

"That's right. That's where they send the 'cores' of the Undying that the Church captures. Miraculous stones, masses only as big as a fist, containing a tremendous amount of ultrapure energy material—their inner structure is a mystery, but as I just told you, scientists are gaining an understanding of how they function. Before, they would capture the entire living Undying"—the man interrupted himself to joke that "living Undying" was a bit of a contradiction as he picked up the pot—"but there was an accident eight years ago when a test subject went berserk, and there were casualties. Since then, we've taken out just the 'cores,' and focused our research on reproduction."

A short, meaningless sound emerged from Harvey's mouth before his voice stopped working.

It wasn't as if he couldn't understand what the man was saying. He knew that the Church had been collecting the cores as relics of the pre-War energy culture, and by extension, he could naturally comprehend that they were trying to get the pre-War technology from them.

But—

"Reproduction...?"

*Of what? Why?* He wanted to continue, but he swallowed his questions. He didn't have to ask. He could guess the answer himself. But it was like his latent consciousness refused to put it into definite words—he didn't want to acknowledge the answer.

The man turned around, an aluminum mug in each hand. The white steam rising from the cups fogged the lens of his monocle, obscuring his focus. He directed an uncertain gaze that seemed to look straight at him, but also to look at the empty space in front of him, and headed toward Harvey.

Harvey unconsciously backed away half a step, and the man offered the cup in one of his hands. The words Harvey didn't want to hear flowed right out of his mouth. "If core reproduction becomes a reality, that means they will be able to create Undying."

He felt dizzy.

That instant,

"___!"

The tinkerer's hand flashed in the shadow of the mug. Harvey pulled instinctively away, and immediately the *thing* in the man's hand charged in his direction. Before he could think, his reflexes kicked in, and he knocked the man down with a right elbow to the side of his head. *Something* brushed in front of his face, sending a strange chill down his spine.

The mug fell to the floor with a high-pitched sound, and coffee splattered out. At the same time, Harvey's assailant crashed backward into the worktable, and everything on it clattered to the floor.

"What…" He stood frozen in a cold sweat for a second, but then got out, "What are you trying to do, damn it?"

He strode over to the man sprawled under the worktable; the tinkerer tried to stagger to his feet, but Harvey stomped on his wrist. He let out a broken scream, but held tight to the thing in his hand, refusing to let go. It resembled a small gun, but its mouth had a wide, elliptical shape, and however he looked at it, it was no more than a handmade toy. What did he think he could do with a thing like that? The man *was* up against an Undying, much as Harvey really hated to think of himself that way.

Still prostrate on the floor, the man raised his face. He clung to Harvey's ankle with his free hand and plastered an insane, twisted smile on his cheeks. "Share your heart…with Elena.…"

"Let go!"

He shuddered and automatically lifted his foot; in that second, the man jumped to his feet and thrust the strange-looking gun at Harvey. "Come on, a little thing like that—" He pulled back and parried with his arm; as he brought his hand back, he tried to grab the gun and take it away, but…

*Vnn…!*

There was a low sound, like a gauge needle spinning past the red zone, and a strange sensation ran across Harvey's palm. It was like being sucked in and blasted in the opposite direction at the same time—it was difficult to describe the unstable feeling that started at his left hand and passed through his entire body like a wave.

"…Huh?"

His knees crumpled.

He tottered a few steps behind him and fell backward onto the rubble.

Harvey didn't realize right away that he had fallen. When he did, he still didn't have the energy to get up. He sensed the man standing in front of him, but he couldn't even turn his head. Still buried in debris, he somehow managed to move his eyeballs and shift his gaze; the man stared at the weapon (Harvey guessed it was a weapon after all) in his hand, muttering something with a look of dissatisfaction on his face.

"So it didn't completely stop him. There's still room for improvement...."

"Damn...you...."

It took a lot of effort to wring those two syllables from his throat. He just barely lifted his head a few centimeters and glared up at the lunatic, who turned his gaze on Harvey and let out an impressed, "Oh?" A dangerous light filled his monocle. "If I shoot you again, will it finally stop you from moving?"

*You're asking me?* Harvey wanted to spit, but as he didn't have the energy to spare to say it out loud, he gritted his teeth without a word.

"It's no big deal; I just want you to hold still for a while," the man said as he crouched down and pushed the gun's muzzle against him. He felt a cold, metallic sensation through his shirt. A little to the left of the center of his chest, right above his core.

*I guess I'll head back for now.*

The words he'd thought before he came down from the flight deck floated into his head. *That's right, I have to go home. There are things I have to apologize for, and a lot of things I need to talk to her about, and then something I have to decide—*

The sensation from before pierced the center of his body.

He heard the dull *thud* of his head hitting the floor, and the world stopped.

# CHAPTER 5

"LET'S GO HOME."

Kieli was sure it was the biggest tombstone on the planet, the oldest tombstone on the planet, and the tombstone that had come the farthest distance.

And she was sure that it just suddenly fell from the sky one day and was erected in an instant.

It was the tomb of the spaceship.

Under the sand-colored sky, the South-hairo wilderness stretched as far as the eye could see, dotted with the pieces of the wreckage of the giant structure that stuck out here and there. Metal walls that had peeled off; the torn, scattered pieces of the tail; something resembling a mangled fuel tank.... A forest of wreckage covered the area, so gigantic she couldn't see the top of any piece of it without lifting her head and squinting, and when she looked up at it, she felt like she had gotten lost in a cemetery of giants.

She actually was at a loss.

She sat next to the bike, holding her knees and playing with the goggles around her neck in place of the radio.

"Aaah…"

She sighed at the distant sky. She focused directly ahead of her; and far in the wilderness, beyond the light haze of gas, she could see a flock of gray chimneys. It was the cluster of exhaust pipes that stood tallest at the very top of town. Those exhaust pipes formed the border where the fault dropped, and the mining town clung along it.

Suzie had lent her the goggles along with the bike, with the instructions to put them on when she got out of town. They had belonged to Buzz, and when Kieli wore them, they covered even her nose and could not have been more of a nuisance. But, just as Suzie had warned her, as she drove across the wilderness, she stirred up tremendous clouds of sand and dust, and things could have been vicious without the goggles. When she looked in the side mirror a second ago, the shape of the goggles stood out clearly on her face, and under those marks, her face was completely black. She found running water next to a parked three-wheeled truck, so she scrubbed her face and took a drink of water while she was at it.

While she had traveled the wilderness, she had gotten completely used to the rusty, sandy taste of the dirty water—come to think of it, she didn't think he realized it himself, but Kieli had noticed long ago that Harvey had an unconscious habit of wiping his face with his shoulder instead of his sleeve.

*Are you here, Harvey...?*

She turned her head, still holding her knees, and looked up at the barrier towering behind her. A rusty metal wall jutted up from the ground and stood blocking her way, as if it was the end of the world. She suddenly thought that the world might not really be round, but more like a room, surrounded by high walls.

Of course, if she looked up at it from a little farther away, she could tell that it was the body of the spaceship poking out of the ground.

There was a truck parked there, so she'd figured that someone must be inside, but when she called out, there was no sign of her voice reaching the interior. When she tried to go inside, she couldn't find a crack to go in through anywhere she could reach, let alone an entrance.

After wandering around the wall for nearly an hour, she still had no idea what to do, and went back to where she had parked the bike. When she got there, someone was sitting in the driver's seat. She gaped for a second and backed away, but the person didn't do anything or even react to her, only gazed absently at the rubble of tombstones spread out before them.

She couldn't move the bike even if she wanted to, so Kieli crouched down a little way off, and was at a complete loss for a while.

"Um...." She tried addressing the person on the bike, giving him a sideways glance as she pointlessly adjusted the band on the goggles.

"Did you come here on this...?"

The shadow only cast his expressionless gaze at the wilderness before him and didn't betray the slightest reaction, as if he didn't notice that she was there.

He was a thin man wearing simple beige clothing. A metal plate engraved with old letters and numbers had been sewn into his sleeve, and a small plate with the same numbers ate into the skin on his cheek.

"...Doesn't that hurt?" she asked innocently.

The man, still directing his downcast eyes forward, muttered, "No, not really." He'd finally responded, and Kieli breathed a sigh of relief.

"I did something really bad and got arrested, so they put it on me and sent me out into space."

"You did something bad?"

"Yeah. I tried to kill someone important."

"You don't look like you'd do that," she said honestly, and then the man looked her way for the first time. He blinked with the faintest of surprise.

"...You think so?" As he smiled wryly in self-derision, his

air resembled a certain someone she knew very well, and Kieli couldn't help looking down. By the time she raised her eyes again, the man was nowhere to be seen.

"Ah…" There was no way anyone could have been sitting there to begin with. The deserted three-wheeled bike just stood there, exposed to the wilderness wind—but in his place, a small metal plate had fallen directly under the driver's seat. Her fingers scratched the ground as she picked it up. It was so rusty, the lettering was almost impossible to distinguish, but Kieli could just barely make out pieces of the numbers from the plate that had been buried in the man's cheek.

*I should have asked him how to get in.…*

She turned back to the starship behind her, feeling a little regret, when, *clunk!* There was a heavy sound, and a crack ran through the wall where nothing had been before.

"Wah…" Kieli's jaw dropped, and she watched as the wall floated up like a sliding door, creating a rectangular opening.

She saw a beige back go inside the gloomy, gaping hole, but he was only halfway through before he literally disappeared.

His hand entered his vision and slid an ID card through a scanner on the wall.

*……? That's not my hand.*

It wasn't the hand he was used to seeing. It was smaller, the hand of a young girl. Apparently the ID card was accepted, and the metallic door slid to the side. When he ducked and peered inside, he couldn't see very far into the room, cluttered as it was with cabinets buried in paperwork, some kind of machine parts, monitors, and countless other things. He discovered the back of a small man in front of one of the desks, half-buried in materials and data.

"Brother!" Of course the voice he used to call out wasn't his own, but that of a girl.

The man turned around. His face was much younger than the one Harvey knew, and more than anything, that strange monocle wasn't attached to his face, which is why Harvey didn't know who the man was for a second. When he called out "Elena!" though, the familiar name connected the dots in his memory.

"Wh-what are you doing here?" the man immediately whispered in a panic and ran toward the girl. He pulled her inside, ran a quick gaze around the hall outside, and closed the door. "How did you get in here?"

"My friend's brother is a plumber, and he said he had work to do in this building, so I had him bring me here in secret. And look. This is your spare ID card."

"That's no reason to sneak all the way in here...."

"I brought you lunch. You're busy today, right?" the girl's voice said brightly, not caring a bit about the man's agitation, and her hands held out the basket she had brought with her. "You almost never come home, even though you promised that we would have breakfast and tea together. What's this?" She interrupted herself, peering at a terminal on the desk. A three-dimensional image of a rough sphere showed on a seventeen-inch display monitor.

"Never mind that, just go home now. There'll be big trouble if they find you."

He blocked her view and the girl reluctantly left the terminal, asking something else instead.

"When is your next vacation?"

"Oh, next week, I think."

"Really? Oh, good. Next Wednesday is the anniversary of Mom and Dad's death."

"...Oh. That's right. Yes, I'll definitely take the day off." The man relaxed his tone a little—for the first time, he showed a normal, pleasant smile, and Harvey was surprised to see how well it suited him. He accepted the basket and held it up to show Harvey, or actually the girl.

"Let's eat before you go. When we're done, you're going home."

"Okay. Okay!"

He felt the girl's emotions as she nodded twice and felt as if he might be glad with her; he had mixed feelings about this.

At the man's urging, the girl cheerfully started to sit in a chair, but suddenly, he heard a door opening behind them. "Ack!" The man pushed her head down and forced her under the desk, then his legs stood in front of her, as if to cover her eyes.

"How's it going, Daniil?"

"H-hi. How are you?" Apparently one of his colleagues had come in, and the man returned the cheerful greeting evasively. Harvey wondered if "Daniil" was the man's name.

"How is the design for the replica going?"

"I think I can miniaturize an entire power plant's worth."

They both sighed; that was nowhere near good enough.

"It really is a tremendous crystallization of lost technology.

Just how did they fit an inexhaustible supply of ultrapure energy into that tiny stone?"

"What about the cell-repairing function?"

"It's a total black box, but it looks as though we can replicate it."

"So it looks like the biggest problem really will be controlling the energy."

Ignoring the difficult-sounding exchange behind her, the girl crawled out to the other side of the desk. Three monitors larger than the one on the desk lined a corner of the room, and they all showed what looked like different angles of the same place. Still crouched on the floor, the girl looked curiously up at the monitors.

The screens were crowded with giant machines, pipes, and cables, and from just one glance, she had no idea what they were showing. But when she looked closely—though she couldn't make it out clearly because it almost seemed to be a part of the machinery—there was a person buried in the center of the equipment. The bundles of cables sprouting from all over his body pulsed in time with his heartbeat—the girl's impression was conveyed directly to Harvey. In her confusion she associated it with the electricity experiments and rat dissections she had done at school. It was so much like an experiment that it didn't really sink in that it was a person there, and the girl thought of him as a different creature. *I wonder if it's alive. I wonder if that hurts. I wonder what it feels like for your heart to move while hooked up to all those things.*

With his head hanging, the silhouette's shoulder suddenly twitched. There was no way he could have noticed her looking at him through the monitors, but he lifted his head slightly and glared her way.

*I know him...!*

"Eek! He looked at me!"

By the time the thought occurred to Harvey, the girl, still on all fours, had flipped around in surprise, and the monitors were in his blind spot. *Wait, wait! Don't run away! Let me see it again!* But no amount of wailing would make it so he could interfere with the girl.

"Elena, what are you—"

"Who's the girl? How did she get in!?" The sound of something breaking overlapped the cries of the man and his colleague. Next, the floor shook like in an earthquake, and the lights in the ceiling flickered a few times. Then all the lights in the room, including the large monitors and the display on the terminal, went out.

One second later, the greenish emergency lights crept up dimly from close to the floor. There was a commotion out in the hall.

"What's wrong? What happened?"

The colleague flew out the door. "Stay here, Elena. Understand?" the man said to his sister before following him. Left behind, Elena cowered on the floor in a daze, but after looking around the room, in the end, she dashed into the hall after the man.

That instant, someone rammed into her. She clung to the wall, nearly falling.

"The specimen has gone wild...!"

"Who activated it!?"

She heard yells and screams down the hall, and lots of people came running, as if fleeing something. Conversely, there was another group heading the other way, violently shoving the confused wave of people aside. The girl joined the latter group and started to run. She was technically an intruder herself, but it seemed now was not the time for anyone to care.

She passed through a few halls and doors and stood at her destination. The scene that entered her view made Harvey think for an instant that she was still looking at the display on the monitors—or actually, that the girl's feelings and his feelings had blended together, and he could no longer tell whose were whose.

In the long, narrow space, buried in giant machinery, Harvey could see the shadow of a large man against the opposite wall. He ripped the cables off his body and punched the equipment around him with his bare fists. "Seize him!" "Bring the guns!" "He's coming this way." "Run!" "Uwaah!" "Help!" In the midst of the black smoke and sparks, people ran in chaos from the grotesque figure of the large man staggering toward them, dragging cables behind him. Screams cut short filled the air.

Still not understanding what was happening, the girl was almost trampled in the panic around her, but she finally found the man she was looking for through a gap in the stampede and breathed a sigh of relief.

"Brother...!"

The man reacted to her voice and turned around. "Elena, no!" he shouted, his eyes suddenly wide. The girl didn't know what was wrong; she thought he was angry that she had followed him as she lifted her face in the direction indicated by his gaze.

A beam was falling from the ceiling, lights and all—Harvey

was probably the only one who realized this immediately. The girl just stood where she was, unable to grasp the situation right away, and looked up at the scene of the rapidly approaching rubble that had once been the beam and its lights, as if it somehow didn't concern her.

*Idiot, run!*

As the girl's feelings blew away, the scene before Harvey's eyes blurred and blacked out, like a monitor being turned off.

His consciousness was abruptly pulled back to reality.

"......!"

Instinctively, he tried to jump up, but his body wouldn't respond, and all that happened was that his fingers moved a little.

A gloomy ceiling, its metal planks peeling off in places, rose above his head. There was no sign of lights having fallen to the ground; rather, the scenery was completely different than it had been in that room.

*Was that...?*

After staring in a daze at the pattern of rust on the ceiling for about ten seconds, Harvey remembered his situation. He had been shot with a strange gun and had passed out—there was no feeling in his body, as if his nerves had been ripped out, and he felt as though he was floating. Fortunately his head was still functioning properly...he thought. He didn't really trust his own judgment today, though.

*To think the cores had such a weakness,* he grumbled inwardly. He imagined that gun (?) was made to temporarily generate something like the magnetic fields created by the fossil fuel strata—no, a stronger magnetic field—and paralyze his core's functions. A sensation similar to the discomfort he felt when going through the tunnel to the abandoned mine in Easterbury had run through his body, followed by a complete loss of strength.

*That's much more effective than a carbonization gun. Scary...,* he thought honestly. He never wanted to get shot with that again.

Harvey didn't think he had been out for very long, but he had completely lost consciousness, so he couldn't rely on his sense of time. He moved his eyes around the area and confirmed the situation. He had been shoved carelessly into a crack in a broken machine or something and lay faceup in an extremely awkward position with his hands and legs sticking out.

*Ugh. What the hell...?*

He looked down at his body and wanted to vomit.

There was a hole a few centimeters across in the center of his chest, as if it had been drilled there, and a bundle of organic cables protruded from the bloody opening.

His senses were numb, so he didn't feel any pain. But as a consequence, he was able to observe with a cool head and was once again disgusted at his own construction, so obviously different from normal people. *I'm still alive after this?* he spat at himself inwardly and averted his eyes. He remembered someone saying the same thing to him before.

Instead of looking at himself, he traced the path of the cables sticking out of him. There was no doubt the man who had drilled the hole used those same bloody hands to handle the cables, and the blood-stained bundle wriggled around the wreckage of machines to the top of his head, like snakes twined together.

He somehow managed to lift his chin; the instant he tried to look up, the rubble under his head crumbled and his neck snapped back, and, conveniently, he could see over his head. But now up was down.

He could see the upside-down back of the man a little way off. Daniil—that was his name.

Something was buried in the inside wall. Harvey furrowed his brow and squinted.

It was a warped ball—it looked similar to a clump of scrap metal that had been compressed for disposal—with things he thought were electrical outlets sticking out all over it, and it had a huge mass of biocables connected to it like tree roots. He had seen something like it before—no, it couldn't be. It was too big.

Even stranger things lined the wall directly above (no, he corrected his sense of direction)—rather, directly *below* the strange sphere. A group of cylindrical capsules, big enough to fit a human—it was his first time seeing any, but he wasn't very surprised. Intellectually he knew that the interstellar space-ships had technology for something called "cryogenic sleep." They said that back in the pioneering era, people would cross vast space, spending decades or centuries in deep freeze. The story of the Saints the Church taught boasted that the Eleven Saints and Five Families, or whatever they were called, took ages to arrive at this planet, but to them it probably just felt as if they had gotten here after a little nap.

Anything remotely useful had likely been carried off long ago, so the capsules that remained were almost beyond recognition. However, just one of them, though distorted, had been repaired. The glass had been patched up with metal planks and was hard to see through, but he could make out the almost too-white face of a frozen person. A girl about thirteen or fourteen—*Elena, no!* For a second, the man's bitter cry echoed inside his head.

Several narrow organic cables pierced the girl's hands and feet, a bundle of thicker cables sprouted from her back, and all of them collected together at the sphere overhead. The cables protruding from his own chest were hooked up to the same ball.

*Huh...*

He was starting to see the connection.

"Hello. So you're awake." Harvey heard the man's monotone voice and shifted his gaze; his eyes met the monocle looking diagonally down at him. Beyond it, he saw Daniil's upside-down face.

"...Yo," he rasped back. He still couldn't get any energy to his vocal chords.

"You reactivated sooner than I expected. How do you feel?"

"Bad," he spat indifferently, indicating behind the man with his eyes, wordlessly demanding an explanation. The man seemed to guess his meaning immediately. He moved over a little to show Harvey and looked up behind him.

"A replica of an Undying's core."

"It's huge...."

Harvey looked up over the man's shoulder in disgust at the object he spoke so proudly of. He had guessed that was probably what it was, but still, it wasn't a replica so much as a copy enlarged a few dozen times, and its quality that much worse for it.

"Even so, this is the very smallest I could make it. With our current technology, it would be impossible to collect all the core's functions into something small enough to fit inside a human body. When I was at the lab, I tried taking an Undying's core and putting it directly into another corpse, but I couldn't control the energy, and the body exploded."

*Exploded.* What the hell were these guys doing? The man even smiled a little as he explained; Harvey felt so much hatred for him and his lab that he wanted to puke, and at the same time, he shuddered to think that something so dangerous was inside his own body.

"I'm going to take some of the energy from your core and give it to my replica. I only need a little. Then I can bring Elena back to life."

"Are you stupid...?" Harvey inquired listlessly, since he still had no energy for his voice—though he probably would have said it the same way under normal circumstances. "Even if it works, she won't come back to life. She'll just move. She'll be hooked up to a weird giant machine and move like a robot, and that's all...." As he murmured this in fragmented bursts—longer statements were still hard on him—he started to doubt his own sense of self. Maybe he didn't have any more "self" than this girl would.

"If her soul goes back inside the moving flesh, then Elena will come back to life. I don't see a problem," Daniil answered in an empty voice, as if what he said was obvious. Maybe it would be more accurate to say his voice sounded automatic. "Now, come here, Elena. You can go back to your body soon."

He called the girl's name and ran his monocled gaze around the empty space. The girl's spirit was nowhere to be found in his sphere of vision, and after looking around once, his eyes stopped on the capsule. He practically danced to it, as if carried away in his fervor; he pressed his face on the glass and peered in at the girl's body.

"Be patient just a little longer, Elena. When you're alive again, we'll have tea together. And eat together. I promised you, after all. I'm sorry I made you wait eight years...."

If what Harvey had seen happened eight years ago, then this man of undistinguishable age really wouldn't be an old man yet. Had a mere eight years done this to him? Well, Harvey supposed that might be a long time to a normal person, but still.

"We can be together forever now. You'll never die again...."

Harvey stared at the man muttering and clinging to the capsule and started to consider something, but immediately turned the thought away as something he didn't want to think about.

Instead, he shifted his gaze behind the man, to the empty space there.

At some point the girl's ghost had appeared in the air and was staring over the man's shoulder at the body contained in the capsule. A frozen corpse, wrapped in cables and looking like an animal from an experiment, with the same face as the ghost herself.

*... Would she be happy to come back to life like that?* he asked himself, and the girl's spirit slowly turned her head. She looked at Harvey with dark, lonely eyes, as if she wanted to say something. Come to think of it, hadn't she been making that face the whole time he had been there?

*Oh. Sorry I didn't get it right away....*

He sighed and lightly closed his eyes. *You wanted to stop him, didn't you? Got it.*

He opened his eyes and looked around; he confirmed that the radio was lying at the edge of his still upside-down vision. If he shifted over a little and stretched out his hand, he thought he would be able to reach, but right now, he didn't even have the energy for that.

*...Don't keep synching with me. I know you can move by now,* he muttered inwardly and waited a few seconds. The fingers on his right hand twitched in response, and he heard the faint sound of a motor from around his elbow. Maybe it was because his nerves had completely fused with it recently; his right arm had apparently followed suit when Harvey could no longer move and ceased all function, but really, it should be able to move independently of him. *What are you doing passing out with me at a critical time like this, damn it...?*

The five metal-framed fingers traced over the machine wreckage like the legs of a beetle and crawled to the radio. They caught the radio's cord as it hung to the floor, and pulled the casing closer.

*Wah, don't face it this way; you're scaring me. The other way, the other way!*

The fingers adjusted the direction of the speaker—

*...Okay, good.*

—and turned on the power.

That instant, the staticky features of a soldier burst from the speaker.

"—mn you!"

The soldier howled, and at the same time, a shock wave shot from the radio with an air-splitting roar. "What in the...!?"

As Daniil turned around, it brushed over his head and scored a direct hit on the giant iron clump of the core replica.

An explosion and a collapsing wall—Harvey couldn't tell which came first. The wall, now rubble, and the iron mass, now covered in flames, collapsed over Daniil's head. He watched it out of the corner of his eye as he gritted his teeth and tried to somehow pull himself up.

Just then, through the cables piercing his chest, he felt an intense suction, as if his heart was being yanked out—and not just his heart, it was enough to make him think every organ inside his body had been carried off.

His vision and hearing went blank for a second, and the world plunged into nothingness.

*Snap...*

He heard the sound of something cracking in the middle of his body.

After that, the noise around him came back all at once. Just as he noticed a low moaning sound and vibrations resounding from under the floor, they immediately reached the walls and ceiling, and the shaking started to envelop the entire room. Was the ship itself shaking?

The next instant, he heard a ferocious roar from somewhere. If he had to describe it, it was a crunching, like a giant excavator boring into the ground. "Gah!" An upward thrust sent him a meter above the floor. He hit it again a second later, and the floorboards, which must have turned brittle, fell out from under him with a spectacular crash.

Harvey opened his mouth to scream he didn't even know what, but whatever it was, he didn't have the time to get it out, as he fell to the empty space below, taking the surrounding rubble and floorboards with him.

She was walking up the gloomy hall, wondering anxiously if she was going the right way, when suddenly everything around her started shaking and rattling.

Fortunately, a handrail passed all the way along the hall walls, so when a bunch of rubble slid down the sloping hall and passed by her, and when her body was flung into the air for a second, and when there was a sharp crash after that, Kieli clung desperately to the handrail and managed to escape disaster. She couldn't imagine that suspensions in midair like this happened very often, so she wondered why the wall would have a handrail. But anyway, it saved her.

The intense quaking and roaring was still going on. Relying on the rail to get her through the shaking, she pressed her face to a crack in the wall and strained her eyes to see what was happening outside.

"It-it's running!" she gasped involuntarily.

The spaceship that was supposed to be sticking out of the ground was sprinting along, its bottom scraping the ground, sending up clouds of sand and dust. *But if a spaceship is running across the ground, then it isn't a spaceship, is it? Er, I mean, I thought this ship was a wreck that stopped being able to move a long, long time ago!*

"What's going on...?"

As Kieli looked in confusion to either side of her, faint static reached her ears. She gasped and looked for the direction the sound had come from. The rubble that slid down had piled up behind her (a little while ago, it would have been down the slope, below her, but now that the spaceship had leveled out and started running, it was behind her), and there was a small hill of debris blocking her path.

She noticed muffled static from a gap in the rubble and she tried to run to it but tripped in the shaking and fell. She used the handrail to pull herself up and traveled back down the hallway, still holding on to it.

Kieli knelt in front of the pile and desperately pushed rubble aside. She strained to pick up a thick metal plank that seemed to be the remains of a wall and pushed it aside, and when she dug up the smaller fragments of metal piled behind it, she found the casing of a small radio buried in the wreckage.

She pulled it out and held it up in both hands.

"Corporal! Corporal!" she called out, shaking it unthinkingly.

"...*Don't shake me,*" a hateful voice came from the speaker mixed with bursts of static. "...*Huh? Oh, Kieli, it's you.*"

"Corporal...I'm so glad. I'm so glad to see you...."

Kieli hugged the radio in her arms and sank to the floor. She put the speaker to her forehead, felt the familiar faint static, and almost cried with relief.

"*What happened? Where are we?*"

"Where's Harvey? He's not with you?"

They simultaneously blurted mismatched questions, and simultaneously fell quiet. After a period of silence, they continued:

"*What's happen—*"

"Where's Harvey?"

They had spoken over one another again, but this time

Kieli's voice was stronger. *"Hell if I know!"* the radio suddenly shouted in reply.

*"This time I really am done with him! Do you know what he said about you? There's no way in hell I'm letting him take care of you any—"*

"Corporal, answer my question!" Kieli interrupted, in a voice sharper than she had intended. She grabbed the radio in both hands and held it to her face. "What happened to Harvey? He's not with you?"

*"I told you I don't know. And you don't have to forgive that son a bitch, either...."*

"Corporal."

*"......"* The speaker faltered, as if she had intimidated him.

"Hey, let's stop. I don't like this. Things are just weird right now, you know? They'll go back to normal soon, right? You said it yourself, Corporal. You said you trust Harvey. I came to find you both. I came to find you and Harvey, both."

*"Kieli..."*

"Let's all go home together. All three of us, together."

*Let's go home.*

He felt as though he heard someone's voice. Maybe he had only muttered it himself.

He pushed aside the steel frames piled on his back and crawled out of the debris, then bent over and coughed two or three times. Some of his feeling had returned, but he still couldn't move decently. Annoyed at himself, he used his right arm to pick himself up, and spotted the bundle of cables piercing his chest.

*Ugh, I'm still connected...?*

Harvey cursed and grabbed the cables in his left hand, but

as he lacked the composure to handle them with care, they snapped as he yanked them out. A pain so intense it made him nauseous ran through him, and he ended up facedown in the rubble again. "This...sucks...." Some of the severe sense of loss from before—the feeling that his heart was being sucked out—was still oddly present with him. And then there was that sound he'd heard right afterward, the sound of something cracking. It couldn't possibly mean...could it?

*You've got to be kidding me....*

He couldn't work up the nerve to check inside his own body himself, so he grabbed his shirt and pulled it together, his forehead still pressed against the rubble.

Collapsed metal planks and steel frames enclosed the area around him, and he had only a narrow field of vision, but it looked as if he had fallen with the floorboards to the lower level of the ship. Under the debris, he still felt intense shaking and heard the moaning of an engine—the ruin was moving. Of course he had no idea what was going on or why, but he could be sure of that one fact.

"Elena...Elena, where are you...?"

He heard a voice muttering on the other side of the rubble and squinted to see through the mangled steel frames. The monocled man, Daniil, was crawling through the debris, pushing aside pieces of the wrecked walls.

"Hey! You!" Harvey shouted, trying to stand. But he broke off with a groan as his legs faltered and he fell, leaving him with no choice but to use just his arms to cross the metal framing and crawl toward the man.

"Why are we moving? Didn't you say that you couldn't create enough power to move the ship!?"

"I said I couldn't do it with the dregs of resources we have now, didn't I? The replica's explosion must have caused the energy in your core to flow backward into the power sector. I didn't make anything but hasty modifications on the engine; there's no way it can control such high energy. Honestly, you Undying—" Daniil maintained his calm expression without resting his hands from moving rubble aside. But as he spoke, his tone rose and his voice grew shrill: "You Undying really are clumps of bottomless energy! It's a terrible shame! To think that if I had been born before the War like you, I could have seen the lost technology with my own eyes!"

"You keep babbling nonsense," Harvey began, then noticed that something was wrong with the man.

A bloodstained iron rod stuck out of Daniil's back. A bent iron pole pierced his side and went straight through his back, probably the remains of the ladder that led to the flight deck. The lens of his monocle had broken, too, and it appeared not to be functioning anymore.

"Hey..." But Daniil showed no sign of concern for his own condition, merely muttering as if possessed while he kept moving rubble aside. "Elena, Elena..." He finally found the girl's body under the ruined capsule. He dug her out and held her lovingly to him. "Oh, Elena. Here you are...." Thrown out of its frozen state, the girl's white body drooped limply against the man's shoulder.

Harvey was chilled by the clearly psychotic scene, but for some reason, he just couldn't look away from the sight of those two—the man and the corpse.

*Get back. It's dangerous....*

He heard a voice whisper beside his ear. The instant he turned to look, the girl's face, so close she touched his cheek, vanished; the next second—

*Whoom!* There was a piercing roar, and the air shook; as he watched, the pile of rubble beneath Daniil's feet fell out from under him. Daniil, the ladder sticking through his side, and Elena's corpse all tangled together as the collapsing rubble took them with it.

Rather than get back as Elena had warned, Harvey reflexively leaned forward, and although he didn't consciously give his arm the order, it reacted and grabbed the falling ladder. The weight of two people and the ladder itself, plus the heaviness of all the rubble beneath them, was enough to pull his arm off, and he heard an unpleasant *snap* somewhere very close—from his arm or his shoulder or inside his head.

Apparently the avalanche of debris had broken through the outside wall. His vision shook with the intense vibrations, and what he saw below him was the wilderness, racing by at incredible speed, the sand and dust it threw up, and the side of the spaceship as it plowed across the ground. He felt dizzy for a second, then immediately pulled himself together.

"Hey, if you can move, then get up here!" he shouted. He wasn't sure if it was fortunate or unfortunate, but with the iron pole skewering him, Daniil was stuck halfway down the ladder. If Harvey reached out his other hand, he might have just barely been able to grab on to the edge of his clothes, but of course he couldn't afford to do that. It was all he could do just to cling to the tear in the outer wall and keep from sliding down himself.

Maybe Harvey's voice reached him or maybe it didn't, but

Daniil had no ears for Harvey as he strained to reach out to the girl's body, caught a few steps below.

"Elena! Elena, grab hold! Elena!"

"Are you stupid!?" *That's a CORPSE!* he wailed inwardly, annoyed. "Get up here, fast!" He wouldn't last any longer himself. The sinew in his right arm had been creaking strangely for a while now. And just then, the metal structure of his prosthetic tore off halfway down his upper arm, ripping the fused skin and flesh as it went.

He swallowed the scream that automatically came to his throat, gritted his teeth, and held back the pain. Even so, he couldn't completely suppress the agony of having his arm ripped off. Cables snapped one after another; a few stragglers managed to hold out for a time, stretching to their limit, but with a high *twang*, fissures began to form in them too.

*I'm sorry. It's okay now. Let go....*

The girl's spirit whispered, appearing before him again and bringing her face close. "No," said Harvey without knowing why; his mouth formed the word without conscious thought. The girl smiled and shook her head.

*Thank you.*

Her voice hung in his ears as she lightly changed direction and slid down through the air along the ladder. As she went, her figure melted into the wind and vanished—at the same time, Daniil, who had just succeeded in pulling Elena's body close to himself, fell off the ladder.

Harvey couldn't help crying out, aghast.

Like dolls thrown violently away, the two figures tangled together and crashed into the rubble and iron frames as they tumbled down and were swallowed up by the wilderness beneath him. Clouds of sand and dust billowed below, and in the blink of an eye, they were left far behind as the scenery raced forward.

"Are you done changing? Would you like some coffee?" the small woman asked in a cheery voice as she appeared in the doorway to the living room.

She spotted Beatrix sitting on the sofa, and opened her mouth in a little "oh, my," then went on to smile brightly. "You really are pretty when you clean up."

"... Yeah, well," Beatrix agreed in a contrary tone, bringing her hand to the back of her head and retying her hair.

The woman walked with a cane, and yet she had been moving around taking care of her all night, so much that Beatrix found it annoying. With a "You must feel awful like that," she'd brought some hot water and half-forced her to wash her blood-stained face and hair, even pushed a change of clothes on her; and to top it all off, her right knee was now in a splint and had a bandage wrapped properly around it. Of course Beatrix couldn't make the woman do something so extreme as to sew her severed leg back on, so she'd adamantly refused the offer.

"Are you buying time? Until the Watch or the Church Soldiers get here?" she asked, and cast a cold glance at the door behind the woman.

"Eh?" The woman blinked two or three times, then looked somehow very sad.

Realizing she might cry, Beatrix winced a little and said, "I'm joking." She sighed and leaned back against the sofa. "Anyway, if you're going to report me, now's your chance. Since I can't run away right now," she added indifferently. She still had no feeling below her knee, but in a little while, her leg should connect enough that she could walk minimally.

Still, whether she could walk or not, normally she would never sit in a house with people she didn't know she could trust, casually letting them take care of her and offer her coffee. But today she honestly felt that they could do whatever the hell they wanted. She just didn't care anymore.

*I'm kinda tired....*

She pulled her uninjured leg up onto the sofa and rested her chin on her kneecap. It was relatively comfortable in this town, so she had stayed a long time. But she would probably have to leave it soon, too. She grew bitter at Ephraim for causing this with his outlandish favors, though it was a little late in the game to start feeling that way now. *Where will I go next? I'm alone anyway. I don't really have any goals. It doesn't particularly matter where I go....*

"You're so alike," the woman suddenly muttered as she readied the coffee set on the table.

Beatrix stared blankly at the woman's profile and then answered with a scowl, averting her eyes, "... Yeah, we're alike." She hated herself for knowing who the woman was comparing her to.

That's why she sometimes lectured him. It annoyed her to feel as though she was looking at herself. She figured, in the end, every single one of their kind was fundamentally the same.

Her chin felt a faint vibration through her knee, and at the same time, the coffee set on the table started rattling a little.

She heard a muffled commotion and a roar from outside the living room window. She instinctively put her guard up and looked in that direction. On the other side of the closed curtain, sounds like engine noise and shadows that looked like three-wheeled trucks passed by one after another.

*What...?*

She took a somewhat defensive stance on the sofa and unconsciously ran her eyes around the room as she started strategizing in a corner of her mind about how to get through this with the least damage to the house. That second, a large shadow appeared slowly in the doorway. "——!" She flipped around, but she still couldn't stand. She got up once, only to sink right back down.

Fortunately, it was only the man of the house who had appeared, but he was a big, scary man who made her want to run anyway. Suzie looked at him anxiously. "Buzz, did something happen outside?"

"The ruins are charging this way."

The man's unexpected remark made Beatrix gape along with the woman. "...Huh?" they both asked dumbly.

With an absolute air of seriousness, the man said, "Apparently the ruins of the spaceship are charging this way across the wilderness. If it keeps going, it'll come over the fault and burst right into town. Everyone's running."

"What? I don't understand. 'Ruins'? That's where Kieli went, right?"

In response to his wife's question, the man shook his head as if he didn't get it either.

Beatrix glanced through the opening in the curtains to check on things outside. The first thing she noticed was a three-wheeled bike with a small mountain of bags forced onto its luggage rack, then people carrying similarly large bags, then a three-wheeled truck packed tight with miners. They were all headed the same direction: down the slope.

It was ridiculous, but if she were to assume that it really might be happening—if that giant structure charged from the top of the fault and slid down the slope—there would be a lot of damage not only to the mine, of course, but as far down as the center of town below. She cursed bitterly in her heart. *What in the world did they* do...?

"I hate to ask when I've already caused you so much trouble, but if you have a free car, could I borrow it?" she asked the giant man, looking away from the window.

It was the wife who answered. "You're going to go?" she asked, immediately understanding Beatrix's intention. "You couldn't possibly drive on that leg. I'll go with you."

"It'd be even more reckless of you to try to cross that uneven wilderness with your hip. Normal people don't stand up to wear and tear, so you should take care of yourself. You can just forget about me already. You two need to get out of here."

She used the arm of the sofa to prop herself up and stood on her left leg. She started to put out her right leg and stumbled; the man's thick arm appeared in front of her and held her up.

"*I'll* drive."

"Now, look! Stop meddling already!"

"I'll let you come along while I go pick up Kieli. Got a problem with that?"

She couldn't help faltering, feeling threatened by his low voice and demeanor that looked as if it would snap at her at any second; and as she did, he hoisted her up onto his shoulder without giving her a chance to object.

*I can't do it anymore. I don't want to walk another step.*

*Keep going! Just a little more. Just one more push.*

*"Keep going, keep going." You just keep saying that because there's no way for you guys to keep going anymore....*

*Avalanche on your right.*

Harvey dodged to the left a bit, reacting to the voice, and a metal beam from the ceiling brushed past his right side, falling with a clang.

He glanced sideways at the small mountain of iron framing and shuddered, then reluctantly and unsteadily started walking again. He was in a hall in the lower level of the ship, encircled by debris. He had to at least climb up one more level; if he stayed here, he would be buried alive before long.

He was technically standing on his own feet, but he practically dragged his body forward, holding on to the wall and the rubble. His arm, dangling from a few taut cables, followed after him, sometimes catching on the debris at his feet and seeming annoyed as it shoved the obstacles away by itself. He didn't have the spare energy to shut off the pain, so his arm had been in incredible agony for a while now. His will to react to the pain had abruptly run out, though, and he only thought, *Damn, that hurts,* strangely calmly, in a corner of his consciousness. The hole in his chest had probably already started healing, but he didn't want to look and so left it alone. An ache had been hanging around the heart of his body—where he'd felt the crack.

He'd instantaneously had enough energy sucked out of him to make this giant structure move, even if it was just skipping along the ground, so it wouldn't be strange for there to be a crack or two. (Of course, he couldn't even imagine what would've happened if it had taken all the energy needed to fly into space.)

As for what effect it would have on *him*...

*...Hell if I care.*

Maybe he was just avoiding reality, but he forced that problem out of his head and instead thought about the man who fell.

Why he'd immediately grabbed the ladder, why he'd desperately tried to help him, yelling at him to climb up—somehow, Harvey knew the reason. Trying to revive a dead person as an Undying (and so incompletely, as well) was so incredibly stupid it took him beyond exasperation or sympathy, and no emotions came to him. He didn't even feel like getting mad that he was nearly killed.

But it wasn't impossible that he might someday turn into that man. If Kieli ever...

"......"

He punched the wall, and rubble rained down on top of him.

*Argh, I can never think about anything good when I'm tired....*

He shook the small pieces of debris off his head, and while he was at it, he shook away all the unnecessary thoughts and focused his attention on walking.

The vibrations and muffled motor sound echoing from under the floor; the intermittent sound of crumbling walls and ceiling; the sound of his own irregular footsteps as he progressed, dragging himself more than walking; the pain he felt in his arm when his prosthetic periodically got stuck between pieces of rubble and struggled....He accepted only minor thoughts like that on the surface of his senses as he silently moved his feet forward.

*All right, you're there. You did good.*

Guided by the voices that echoed in his eardrums, he looked up. A faint ray of light shone through a gap in the crumbling ceiling. Metal planks and iron beams piled high; they were unstable, but they were something to stand on, and it looked as if he could manage to climb up.

"...Thanks...for showing me the way," he said, quietly expressing his gratitude to the voices.

He saw two shadows pass through the gap in the ceiling and up to the light. Two men wearing pale blue jumpsuits. The one in back turned around, smiled carefreely, and gave a thumbs-up. The one in front just glanced coolly at him, but then whispered:

*Do the best you can. Even if you do have a long way to go.*

Then he disappeared in the light. "See, that's *exactly* how I paraphrased it!" his friend criticized, then he disappeared after him with one last yell of, "Keep going!"

*... You say it like it's so easy, but it's tiring to keep going.*

He looked down and sighed with a wry smile.

"Harvey."

The voice made him doubt his hearing.

He automatically froze for a few seconds, still facing down, then raised his head somewhat awkwardly.

"Harvey, I'm so glad I found you."

A girl's face peered in through the gap in the ceiling that the jumpsuited men had disappeared through. A radio swung at the end of the cord around her neck.

"...It's...you. Why?" was all he could murmur, his voice hoarse, as he stood there. The white gauze on her forehead stood out painfully under the faint light behind her head, and the dull ache he felt in his heart throbbed sharply for a second, piercing him.

"I came to find you. Are you hurt?"

She was the one who was hurt, but she didn't seem to care about that. She reached out to him, looking as if she was about to cry. "Can you get up? Can you hold on?" As she leaned forward, the fragile gap in the ceiling widened, and part of the ceiling crumbled.

"Ah!"

The girl slid down from the ceiling along with the rubble. "You id..." Moments ago he'd been thinking that he couldn't walk decently anymore, and that he didn't even want to, yet now his body moved automatically. He ran, stumbling, up the pile of debris and caught her in his left arm. As he went on to embrace her head with the same arm, his shoulder slammed into the rubble, and immediately ceiling debris rained on them from overhead.

Harvey was hit on his back, shoulder, and various other places all at once, and all the air was knocked out of his lungs.

"Ow. Look, you…," he grumbled in a whisper as he regained his breath a moment later. "I-I'm sorry." He involuntarily slackened his hold on her and she jumped away, so he immediately grabbed her hand and pulled her back.

He hadn't really put any thought into the action, so he just grabbed her and froze.

"Harvey…?" she asked wonderingly. He held her hand tightly, without a word, his face still pressed against the rubble. It really was a small, delicate hand compared to his. She always desperately reached out this hand for him… and back there on the stairs, he had brushed it away.

"…Sorry," he murmured under his breath. "…I'm sorry. I…"

"Let's go home, Harvey." Her whisper interrupted him, and her other hand hesitantly touched his neck. At the cool, comfortable feel of her palm, he was sure it was his imagination, but the pain throbbing through his entire body softened a little.

A quiet voice, with just a little hint that she might be about to cry, whispered in his ear.

"I came to get you. Let's go home now. Okay?"

He prayed in his heart, to no one in particular, to please let him stay buried in the rubble a while longer. *I can't lift my head. What kind of face am I making now?*

When asked, "So have you thought about how we're gonna get back?" Kieli turned to the crack in the wall and looked outside, gazed at the scenery that raced by, and tilted her head in thought. Harvey didn't look outside, but at Kieli's face, and a faint smile rose to his lips. He strangely seemed to be enjoying himself.

"You knew I couldn't answer when you asked, didn't you?"

"Yup. That's right."

"You're evil," she said with a pout. Normally, it made her happy to see Harvey smile like that because it meant he was in a pretty good mood, but now she got the feeling it was just bravado.

See, he shouldn't have the composure for that. His prosthetic arm was only hanging on by its cables, and while technically it was moving on its own, it didn't appear that the nerves were all connected. His upper arm, where it tore off, as well as the chest area of his shirt were covered in blood, and he sat leaning against the wall with his whole body covered in wounds.

There was one other thing that bothered her. He would sometimes grab his shirt near his heart.

"Harvey, are you really okay...?" Kieli sat diagonally across from him and peered into his face.

"I'm fine. Ah, I'm in a little pain," he answered, surprisingly honestly, and then he reached behind Kieli's head and pulled her to him. He rested his forehead lightly on her shoulder and

murmured in a somewhat drained voice, "I feel better like this...."

Feeling his faint sigh and copper-colored hair on her neck, Kieli sat still in that position for a while. Under their heads, the radio was muttering static. Still unable to contain his rage, the Corporal had almost started yelling again when they found Harvey, but the second he saw his face, "...*What the hell happened to you?*" was all he spat quietly before falling into a sulky silence.

"It's kinda been a long time since we've really talked. About a week, huh?"

"Yeah." Kieli immediately nodded at the voice in her ear. "No, about two days," she corrected, after a little thought.

Harvey only reacted with, "Oh, is that right?" as though it didn't matter.

It was the evening of the day before yesterday that she'd found Harvey and Beatrix at the gambling house and Harvey hadn't come home. Just two days. Now the same old scent of tobacco that had seemed so far away from her in those mere two days was right beside her. She felt such relief, but at the same time, anxiety at the thick smell of blood mixed with it.

"...Kieli, hey. There's something I need to consult you about."

*Consult.* Did Harvey even have such an admirable word in his vocabulary? "Huh? Okay. What is it?" she asked, worrying that he might have gone crazy from massive blood loss.

Harvey seemed to hesitate, and after some silence began, "I think I'm going to..."

The floor they sat on suddenly shot up with a *thunk*, interrupting him.

Kieli's shoulder and Harvey's forehead struck each other lightly. "Ow! I bit my tongue...." Harvey grumbled, holding his mouth, and looked up; but then he opened his eyes wide in shock and stared behind Kieli.

Kieli turned to follow his gaze; at the same time, she heard a destructive rending sound, and the gap in the outer wall ripped wider as part of the wall tore off. The heavy metal wall flew up like a scrap of paper, and blew away behind them in the blink of an eye.

"Whoa..."

On the other side of where the wall used to be, the racing scenery spread wide outside, and the rushing wind and the roar of the ship's bottom scraping away at the ground rang in her ears.

"Wow, nice view," Harvey said unconcernedly and crawled over to (what had been) the outer wall. "Looks like it's gonna keep falling apart. I guess we can't just sit and wait for it to stop on its own...." The wild wind blasted through his hair as he checked the situation outside. As soon as he cast his eyes in the direction they were heading, his expression suddenly froze.

"Crap..."

"Hmm? What?"

Crawling on her hands and knees across the ever-shaking floor, Kieli poked her face out beside Harvey's. "Ah!" On the other side of the barrens before them, a cluster of gray chimneys entered her field of vision. At that instant, a strong gust nearly carried off the radio, along with the top half of her body.

"Moron, stay inside!"

Harvey narrowly managed to wrap his arm around her and

stop her, and they both practically fell into the refuge of the wall's shadow. "Be a little more careful. When you're like that, the worry shakes my resolve to—"

Harvey sighed in mild annoyance over her head and suddenly changed the subject midsentence. "...We're heading straight for town." He plastered his back to the wall and glared at the wilderness ahead. "We fall over that fault, and we won't get out of this safely, either."

"More importantly, the town'll be in huge trouble if a huge ship like this charges through it!" Kieli's face snapped up and she unintentionally spoke in an accusing tone. Harvey sent a look her way and blinked.

"...Oh. Oh, yeah." He only nodded halfheartedly before averting his eyes back outside. Kieli bit her lip, unsure what else to say.

"I'm gonna go look for a way!" Anyway, she couldn't just do nothing. When she turned around and started to stand, he called her name.

"Kieli."

She stopped and turned back, still half-standing. Harvey directed his usual emotionless expression forward and murmured in his hallmark frank tone, "Do you like that city?"

"...Yeah. Pretty much." She had the feeling he had asked her that before. She nodded blankly and Harvey seemed to mutter something under his breath.

"All the controls were carried off, so we can't hit the brakes or change direction. All we can try is to cut off the power..." He trailed off, glancing at Kieli. "No, we can't."

Harvey dropped his head and sighed. "If only you weren't here...."

"What's that mean!?"

Kieli was not happy with the remark, but Harvey said nothing and stayed frozen for a while; after a few moments, he looked up as if he had suddenly realized something. He leaned outside the wall and stared out the way they were headed.

"......?" Kieli peered outside, too, over Harvey's back in order to stay out of the wind.

She saw a small cloud of dust approaching diagonally ahead of them. The ship raced forward at a high speed, and the distance between them shrank in no time, so she was shortly able to determine the identity of the cloud.

It was a small, three-wheeled covered truck.

"Buzz!" she called out automatically. Crammed into the driver's seat, stiffly clutching the steering wheel, was a big man with a beard. Another silhouette poked her face out of the passenger seat window. Her long, golden hair tied behind her, fluttering in the wind, she squinted up at them, then looked back at the driver's seat and shouted something.

The truck kicked up a cloud of dust as it made a one-eighty and started driving parallel to the wall out of which Kieli and Harvey were peering.

Beatrix leaned out of the passenger side and called out to them. Kieli could hardly make out any of it over the roar thundering around them, but she was probably wailing something like, "What are you doing? You're nothing but trouble!"

"Bea, you're the best! This is great timing!" Harvey leaned out, too. He didn't care at all about her complaints and actually shouted praise back at her. As Kieli gaped at his unusually bright voice, he grabbed her shoulder and pushed her forward.

"Take care of her!" She turned back in surprise. "What's going on, Harvey? What are you saying?"

"I'm going to stop it before it hits the town. You get off here."

"No! How can you say that…!?"

"It's okay, you can jump over to the truck. I'll help you. Trust me."

"That's not the problem!" she interrupted, wailing at the top of her voice. Harvey backed away, faltering a little, and she clung to his neck. "I'm not leaving you! Not this time." Something like this had happened before. On the Church Soldiers' train, when they were running from Joachim. She didn't see Harvey for two weeks after that—she never wanted to go through that again.

"Kieli, listen to me."

"I won't listen! Whatever you say, I'm not doing it!"

She shook her head fiercely in response to the persuading voice at her ear and tightened her arms around him.

"Kieli. Please, listen," Harvey repeated patiently, and his sigh caught in her ear. His usual subdued tone, his low, slightly gravelly voice.

"No matter how hard I try, I just can't feel any attachment to that town, and I don't really care what happens to it. I even think it would be great if the ship just kept going and wiped out those Watch guys. That's me personally…but if you like that town, if there are even a few people there that were nice to you, if you say you want to, I want to protect it. I want to with all my heart. So…"

His voice broke off there. He took a breath, as if he was tired from talking, and went on. "So I'll do whatever it takes to stop this thing, if you get off. I can only think of a violent way to do it, and there's going to be a big crash. It's all I can do to take care of myself right now, and I'm not confident that I can protect you. Please, listen to reason."

"...No. Harvey, you..."

"I'll be fine. If I'm alone, I can manage somehow. Okay?"

"...No..."

"Kieli."

"......"

Kieli pursed her lips and hung her head. She loosened her grip just a little and stepped away just a little. She gazed, almost glared, for a time at Harvey's neck in front of her. There were beads of sweat there, dirty with blood and dust.

Slowly, she let go.

"Thanks. Now go," sighed a relieved voice from above her. She glanced back up at Harvey's face one more time as he pushed her shoulder, but Harvey was no longer looking at her.

"Ephraim...!" She heard Beatrix's voice faintly from the truck running beside them.

"Get a little closer! She's coming down!"

She didn't know if his voice reached them, but Harvey gestured instructions, and Buzz turned the wheel and brought the truck right up next to the outer wall. The passenger door opened and Beatrix leaned out, shouting something like, "Are you *serious*?"

His right arm, its cables stretching out of it, held on to her hips like a lifeline, and his left hand supported her, too, as she stepped onto the edge of the wall.

"*Herbie.*" Suddenly a voice leaked out of the radio. "*I'll go with you*," it said shortly and grumpily. Kieli gaped down at the radio, then twisted her neck to look back at Harvey.

Harvey froze for a few seconds, face tight, then said, "... Thanks." He softened his expression slightly and lifted the radio's cord off Kieli's neck. He wrapped the cord around his left hand, then supported Kieli's back again. "You can do this."

"Yeah." Kieli nodded a little nervously as she stared at the ground flying by below her.

"You just have to kick off as hard as you can and jump. You can trust Beatrix. I guarantee it."

"Yeah. I can trust Beatrix."

"All right. Good."

He pushed her. She kicked hard off the wall, and the feeling of Harvey's hand left her. Beatrix leaned as far as she could out of the passenger's seat and stretched out her arms; her fingertips touched Kieli's hands, and at the same time, the lifeline of his right arm left her—also, at the same time, a sideways gust rammed into her. The wind carried her with it, and she flew backward.

"Kieli!"

In the nick of time, Beatrix grabbed her wrist and pulled her into the passenger's seat.

Her face plowed into Beatrix's chest, and they fell into the driver's seat, where Buzz's giant body acted as a cushion, conveniently absorbing the shock. Still, Beatrix coughed painfully, and Kieli immediately jumped off of her.

"Harvey!"

She latched on to the passenger door and looked up at the spaceship rushing beside them. Harvey had crouched at the edge of the outside wall and was pulling in the cables of his right arm with his left hand as it fluttered in the wind. For just a second, he seemed to glance her way and smile a little, but...

*Boom!*

There was a muddled explosive sound behind them, and the truck suddenly lost speed, as if it had caught on something. In no time, it was left behind by the racing spaceship.

The last thing to pass by the truck, shaking the ground violently as it went, was the back of the spaceship, buried in the ground until just a little while ago, its tail torn off. In a daze, Kieli watched the cylindrical ship go, running across the barrens with thick black smoke spewing from its exposed jet nozzles, and thought it looked like a train that didn't run on rails.

"Corporal."

*"Herbie."*

They murmured simultaneously and went quiet simultaneously.

"......"

"......"

After some silence:

"I'm sorry."

*"Sorry."*

They spoke over one another again. After another silence:

"I apologized a second before you. I win."

*"Why you—"*

"Do you have enough power for a really big blast?"

*"I have a reserve of enough power to blast you twelve times."*

"Right now, a little push would be more than enough to knock me over."

*"...Says the man who doesn't know when to kick the bucket. Can you really do this?"*

"I think so," Harvey answered with a wry smile, then, tired of talking, walked in silence for a while.

He had gone to so much trouble crawling out, but here he was, going back down to the lower level's hall, following the rubble as he made his way unsteadily toward the back of the ship. Apparently even when you thought you really couldn't take another step, if you used all the willpower you had, you could still keep walking surprisingly far.

Sometimes debris would come crumbling down as the hall continued to shake, and for a while now, ghosts wearing beige prison clothes had been flying around the air, though they didn't show themselves clearly. They looked as though they were just running back and forth in a panic, but when he came to a fork in the road, they would all slide in the same direction as if showing him the way.

*"Kieli sure is strong. Makes us look like idiots for having a fight over something so stupid."*

"Yeah."

*"She's a strong, straightforward girl who gives everything her all. Seriously, she's too good for you."*

"Yeah. She is too good for me."

It wasn't that Harvey wasn't thinking about his answers, but his responses became somehow mechanical, and there was a little pause before the radio spoke again.

*"Hey. You're thinking about something, aren't you?"*

"...Nothing really."

"*Say it.*"

Intimidated by the low voice, he stared silently at his feet for a few seconds. Every step was extremely heavy; if he didn't focus, he wouldn't be able to go on. Using eighty percent of his nerves to take the next step, he took the other twenty percent to put his thoughts into words.

"...I think it would be better not to hang around Kieli forever like this."

"*She likes things the way they are now. There's no problem here.*"

"Not for Kieli, but for me, there's a big problem. Kieli's got a whole life full of possibilities ahead of her. I don't have the confidence to say it's okay for a guy like me to mess with that, and I'm not ready."

"*You may be a little stupid and immature and insensitive.*"

"Shut up." *Don't talk like Beatrix.*

"*But even so, that girl stays with you because she trusts you. She doesn't have a single doubt.*"

"That's all the more reason. I'd be in trouble if I kept taking advantage of that part of Kieli when I haven't really thought things through, or at least that's what I figure. I want to really think about it for a while, alone."

"*Why are you only ever serious about weird things like that?*"

"Well, excuse me."

"*Sheesh.*"

He thought he might get yelled at again, but all that came from the speaker was a resigned sigh. Radios didn't breathe, but that was the impression Harvey got.

"... *There's no helping your troublesome personality now,*" the radio spat, then said nothing more on the subject.

The ceiling ahead of them had collapsed, and the hall beyond it had become a narrow tunnel. The ghosts swam in the air and disappeared into it, one after another. Harvey followed them and crawled inside on all fours. As he went deeper, the heat and the smell, like old oil, got stronger. Occasionally the ceiling and walls around him would peel away in the shaking, and small pieces of rubble rained on his head.

The sound of the engine gradually grew closer, and when it changed into a low, heavy roar that pounded the core of his head, he came out of the tunnel and into a slightly more open space.

Thick pipes crept closely together over the walls and ceiling with their metal planks half peeled off and converged at the engine in the deepest section of the room. Far inside the complex engine, he could see the burning of a faint amber light—that must be the reactor in its heart. It was hard to suddenly believe that it was possible to move an interstellar spacecraft from the distant mother planet with the resources of *this* planet, but the energy from his core seemed to be working smoothly—or rather, damned inconveniently.

"I'm glad you came with me. Actually, I hadn't really thought of what to do."

"*You want me to blast that thing? But if we're not careful, we won't get out of this in one piece, either, you know.*"

"I'll just run as fast as I can."

"*Not a very good plan...,*" the radio grumbled in exasperation, but immediately changed its tone. "*When I hit it, just get away as fast as you can, and jump somewhere you can hide.*"

"Roger that."

He ducked down, pushed the radio forward, and aimed its speaker directly at the reactor. When he started the count-down in his head, the radio abruptly changed the subject. *"You do plan on coming back, right?"*

Harvey couldn't answer right away. The noise of the engine ate into his thoughts, and he couldn't consider anything too deeply.

He took a breath, then muttered his reply, although the noise around them drowned out his voice and he didn't know if the radio could hear him or not. "...I do intend to come home."

A shock wave burst out of the radio. Its blast flew straight for the center of the reactor at the speed of sound; half a second later, a white light enveloped his vision....

For a second, Kieli saw a white light gush out of the jet noz-zles. The next instant, the back of the starship tore off, became a ball of fire, and rolled away. The detached body of the ship plunged forward quite a ways, jumping along the ground and scattering metal walls around it, then finally turned a revolu-tion and a half and stopped.

After witnessing the event, Kieli leaned out of the passenger seat and squinted impatiently ahead of her until the three-wheeled truck, only able to run at a sluggish pace as it spouted smoke, finally arrived on the scene.

"He is so reckless. What an idiot...," Beatrix muttered absently, squeezed into the passenger seat with Kieli. Detect-ing a serious air in her exasperated voice, Kieli bit her lower lip, her gaze still fixed forward.

When they got to the edge of the wreckage strewn about the

spaceship, she couldn't bear waiting for the truck to stop completely and jumped to the ground.

"Harvey!" she shouted to her right and left as she pushed her
way through the mountain of debris. The one fortunate thing
was that this part of the ship had separated from the power
sector before the fire from the explosion could engulf it, so
there were no flames. She covered her face against the thick
clouds of dust as she looked around, feeling as though she was
praying.

"Harvey, answer me! Harvey!"

"Kieli."

A thick voice came from behind her, and she turned to see
that Buzz had parked the truck and was following after her
over the rubble. He had tried picking up metal walls a few
times along the way, but when he strode up to Kieli, he closed
his eyes regretfully and shook his head. "It'll be hard to find a
single person in all of this. We'll need help."

"We can just take our time digging him out, can't we? He
won't die, no matter how many years he's buried," Beatrix said
in a carefree tone as she came up behind him, dragging her
bad leg. Kieli involuntarily glared threateningly at her, and she
winced. "I get it. I'm joking." She sighed and averted her eyes.
She gazed over the ocean of rubble spreading before them and
bit her shapely lip.

"...Do you hear something?" she muttered abruptly and
stood still, tilting her head as if straining her ears. Kieli blinked
and looked back at Beatrix's face for a second, and then she,
too, focused on her hearing.

What reached her ears were the sound of the wind blowing
over the barrens, and occasionally, the sound of falling debris.

And, in the distance, the wreckage of the power sector crackling in flames.

Through all of those sounds, it was faint, but she definitely
heard something else. It came off and on, so she couldn't quite
make it out—the staticky sound of stringed instruments.

She gasped, looked up, and turned toward the music. It was
in the very back of the severed ship's body, and she was already
running by the time she'd finished processing that thought.
Some rubble caught her foot, causing her to stumble, but she
hurriedly picked herself up and crawled on all fours across the
debris, looking for the place the sound was coming from. She
heard the faint melody only in spurts, so she couldn't get a
clear hold on it.

She desperately searched around her, on the verge of tears.
"Corporal, where are you...!?"

*Rustle*...

Very nearby, under her chin, she heard the sound of rubble
scraping against rubble.

When she dropped her gaze, suddenly, someone else's hand
stuck out from the pile of debris under both of hers. She
instinctively let out a short scream and jumped back. Landing on her rear, she looked again and saw a metal-framed
right hand struggle as it tried to crawl through a gap in the
wreckage.

".....!"

She hurriedly crawled to it and helped the right hand move
the rubble away. Buzz ran over and shifted the metal walls
piled up around her. The faint, muffled noise gradually became
clearer, and under the last metal wall Buzz picked up, she
could see red hair, now white with dust.

"…Harvey!"

He lay buried in rubble and limp as though dead, but his left hand held tightly to the radio, protecting it. Apparently the right hand had crawled out on its own, looking for help, just barely attached by torn cables.

"Harvey, are you okay?" she addressed him and waited a little, but he didn't react.

She burrowed into a gap in the rubble and peered into his face. "I know you're alive. Come on…." She timidly reached out her hand and brushed away the hair on his forehead, and he finally twitched. He slowly opened his eyes, blinked somewhat absently, and sluggishly shifted his gaze toward her.

"…Did it work?"

The instant she opened her mouth, she thought she would burst into tears, so Kieli wordlessly and emphatically nodded her head.

A tiny hint of the smile he had when he was in a good mood rose to the corner of his mouth, and he muttered, "…Heh, heh. We did it." Then he closed his eyes, exhausted.

They saw the Watch's trucks approaching from the direction of town, so they hurried to vacate the area.

There had been all kinds of trouble, so they probably wouldn't be able to go back there. She had been saying "Let's go home" all this time, but that home no longer existed.

It was sad, but for some reason, now she felt as though they had come home to the place they had been before.

Wearing the radio in her usual fashion for the first time in a long while, Kieli smiled to herself. She looked back at the three-wheeled truck parked a little ways off. Harvey sat on the edge of its covered bed, leaning against the side wall, staring into space. His torn arm had been shoved into place and bandaged with a cloth for the time being, and his hands were thrust into his pants pockets. Beatrix was in similar shape. Kieli wished Undyings would take better care of their bodies.

"Kieli, get in. We're leaving," Beatrix said, looking out from the driver's seat. Her bound golden hair flowed over her shoulder.

The small three-wheeled truck that they decided to borrow was the one that had been abandoned where the ruins of the spaceship used to be, and according to Harvey, there was no reason they couldn't use it now.

"I'm coming!" Kieli answered, facing forward again, lifting her chin up as high as she could to see into the face of the big man standing in front of her.

"Thank you for everything. Will you tell Suzie that for me, too?"

"Yeah."

"And tell her I'm sorry I had to leave without seeing her again."

"Yeah. I'll tell her."

A little flustered by Buzz's usual curt reactions, she gave a final bow of her head and finished with, "Really, thank you." When she looked up again, giant hands picked her up effortlessly by the waist.

"Wah!"

He pressed her face to his sturdy neck and hugged her tight.

Kieli put her cheek on that neck that smelled of dust and sweat, and the constant scent of milk and butter, and closed her eyes just a little.

"Take care," came his plain parting words, and he put her back down.

"Kieli, I'm going to leave you here!" a slightly impatient voice urged.

"Coming!" Kieli hurried to turn around. (Beatrix might really leave her behind.) She ran back to the truck and started to climb into the bed; that instant, there was a revving noise and a jolt, and the truck really did set off in earnest.

"Wah, meanie...!"

She panicked, about to be left behind, and Harvey grabbed her with his left hand, just managing to pull her in. She sat on the edge of the truck bed and breathed a sigh of relief as she looked up at Harvey. He didn't say anything in particular, only leaned back against the wall, directing his gaze outside.

The truck immediately sped up, spouting smoke from the exhaust pipe in its rear. Buzz's truck, with Buzz standing next to it watching them go, grew farther away against the wilderness scenery. Kieli leaned out from the truck bed and waved. Buzz answered with a nod, then seemed to smile a little. But he had already gotten much smaller in the distance, so she might have imagined it.

She pulled her legs off the edge of the bed and adjusted her position, watching the scenery as she listened to the sound of the truck's engine and its tires rumbling over the road. She glanced next to her at Harvey. He just leaned against the side wall as his vision drifted over an ambiguous spot in the sky, looking at nothing in particular.

"Harvey," she interrupted him hesitantly, and a second later, he blinked lightly and turned toward her.

"...Oh, sorry. I wasn't listening."

"I haven't said anything yet."

"Oh. What is it?"

"Mmm..." Kieli was somewhat suspicious of his answers—they seemed to indicate a screw loose somewhere—but she didn't say anything about it as she returned her attention to the landscape outside.

Far beyond the wilderness disappearing behind them, several lines of black smoke rose up, as if the sand-colored sky was breathing them in. That was where the power sector blazed on.

"The ruins are gone now...."

"They just changed shape and location a little, that's all."

"...Oh." His simple explanation strangely made sense to her.

The spaceship sticking out of the ground had turned into the wreckage of a spaceship lying on the ground, and it had changed location a little—it was much closer to the city than it had been the day before—but still, it wasn't much different from yesterday, and starting today, *that* place would be the South-hairo spaceship ruins. Kieli got the feeling that if she had the chance to come back a few years later, it would probably still be standing there quietly, one with the land, as if it had been there for hundreds of years.

She hoped that she would be able to come back someday. To the town where Buzz and Suzie lived. The town that had been home to Kieli, even if just for a short while. And the town that Harvey said he wanted to protect.

TRAVELERS TRAVERSING THE PLANET

She woke to the sound of the truck's canopy blowing in the wind.

The clattering vibrations and the noise of the engine reverberated under her cheek on the floor. She was wrapped up in a blanket in a corner of the truck bed; she didn't remember going to sleep, but apparently she had been dozing. Above her head, the radio played staticky music at a low volume that melted into the truck's reverberations.

She opened her eyes a little, confirmed that it was dark around her, and closed them again. She wanted to keep sleeping.

It was their second night driving across the South-hairo wilderness since she'd said good-bye to Buzz. They'd encountered another truck on the way, and its driver was kind enough to share some blankets, water, and food. He saw that at least one of them was covered in blood and dust, and even gave them some clothes to change into.

Just as she was about to fall into the depths of slumber once again, Kieli noticed muffled voices talking in the seats up front. They blended with the rattling of the truck and only reached her as whispers, but they were exchanging short, sharp words, as if they were arguing.

Finally, she heard words like "favor" and "owe," and as the conversation cut off, the truck stopped for a moment. There was the sound of the passenger door opening and closing; then she sensed someone open the back cover a crack and climb into the truck's bed. The sound coming from the radio suddenly disappeared. There were a few seconds of oddly pregnant silence, but then the truck started up again and the familiar staticky music began once more.

"...Harvey?"

"Sorry, did I wake you up?"

"No…"

She rubbed her eyes groggily and sat up. In the darkness, a tall shadow crawled up to her on one hand and sat by the wall. She thought she heard him search his pockets, and a flame sprang to life from his lighter. Harvey's profile rose into view as he lit the cigarette in his mouth.

"…Can I sit by you?"

He didn't answer, but the small light at the end of his cigarette nodded, so Kieli dragged the blanket with her and sat down next to Harvey.

"I just had an interesting dream."

"Huh. What was it about?"

"I'm not telling. It was boring."

"Make up your mind."

After the brief exchange, the conversation immediately broke off.

It was a dream about a long time ago, when she was living with her grandmother in their apartment in Easterbury. In the middle of it, for some reason, her grandmother changed into her mother, and her mother saw Kieli off as she went to school. Becca sat next to her, and the Corporal was the history teacher, but he was still a radio, and he talked from on top of the teacher's desk.

Even she thought it was a pretty wishful-thinking kind of dream. But she wished she could have seen a little more of it. After all, Harvey hadn't shown up yet, and she wanted to see what role he would play.…

She fell into a doze as she thought about it, and her head plopped onto the shoulder next to her.

"Mm. Sorry…"

"It's fine. Sleep. It won't be morning for a while."

He hugged her head lightly toward him and pressed her cheek to his shirt. She felt his fingers gently touch the adhesive bandage on her forehead. "Okay.…" His pleasant warmth and the scent of tobacco enveloped her, and her eyelids naturally grew heavy. She felt as though she could see more of that dream if she went to sleep now, and she accepted the invitation to give herself over to slumber.

"Good night," his low voice whispered in her ear. As sleep pulled her consciousness further away, she wondered why the words sounded like a farewell.

"I think I'll go to the capital. I want to see if Jude is alive or dead."

"The capital's risky. It would be like jumping into a nest of Undying hunters."

"Oh, it'll work out."

"As usual, you haven't thought this through, have you?"

"I have a favor to ask. I want you to look after Kieli for a while."

"What?"

"I'm going alone. I can't take Kieli with me. You take her."

"You've got to be kidding. No. First of all, what are you going to tell her?"

"……"

"You *can't* tell her, can you?"

"…Tell her I'm sorry."

"She'll cry, you know."

"...Yeah."

"...Now, look. If it's enough to have you making that face, just take her with you."

"You're the one who told me to leave her with someone...."

"I told you to leave her with someone, but I never once said that *I* would take her."

"You're the only one I can trust her with."

"Don't count on me only when it's convenient for you."

"Bea."

"I don't care."

"Beatrix."

"...Don't call me that only when it's convenient for you."

"Please."

"...This is a big favor."

"I'll owe you."

A faint, sand-colored light shone through a break in the thick, blue-gray clouds filling the sky overhead.

He stopped and turned around, squinting into the brightening distance. He'd thought he might still be able to make out the shadow of the truck he had left a few moments ago, but as far as the eye could see, all that spread before him was the South-hairo wilderness, barren except for a few forlorn shrubs sprouting here and there. He couldn't even find the faintest cloud of dust.

Harvey breathed a light sigh and dropped his eyes, then he

suddenly remembered something and shifted his gaze to the dirt in front of his shoes.

His shoe took one firm step on the ground, and he wondered if he was standing on a path right now. It was possible that he had set foot on an absurdly wrong path. He didn't have an ounce of confidence that what he had decided today was right.

"... Well, I guess it'll work out." Even so, if he kept walking, he would most likely get somewhere soon enough.

He wanted to try walking alone for a while. He hadn't in a long time.

Still, "alone" before and "alone" now weren't exactly the same....

A small motor moaned somewhere near his right elbow, asserting itself.

"Oh, sorry. That's right; you're with me now."

He looked down at the right hand he had shoved into his pocket and smiled wryly. The right arm was mostly connected now, but the nerves hadn't fused together yet. Somehow, he had a hunch that they might never go back to complete synchronization like before—it wasn't as if he had ever measured it, so this was based only on what he felt, but he thought the regeneration of his wounds was subtly slower now. Very rarely, when he had completely forgotten about it, a dull pain throbbed in the heart of his body.

... *Well, it'll* probably *work out,* he decided. Although even Harvey got the feeling that when it came to himself, he was negligent, or maybe careless, or actually just not thinking at all.

"Guess I'll get going," he murmured, half to his partner and half to himself, then turned on his heels and started to walk again.

The sandy, dry wind blew past, ruffling his hair. He once again felt the wilderness air on his skin, so familiar to him that he was sick of it; and he walked alone as he had done alone for so long: not too fast, not too slow, but at his usual pace.

He noticed that his usual pace was a little slower than it had been before.

He stopped and turned around one last time, casting a glance far across the landscape, beyond the horizon hung with sand-colored gas, to where an old three-wheeled truck most likely rumbled along.

Alone before and alone now were a little different.

This time, he had a place to return home to.

AFTERWORD

Hello, I'm Yukako Kabei.

As I write this afterword, I'm right in the middle of packing up to move, and my apartment is almost a jungle. I've somehow managed to carve out a place to work and a place to sleep— that's all—and I move around by weaving between cardboard boxes, trash bags, and mountains of books I need to throw away. Sometimes cardboard boxes stuffed with books block the doors, and I've been trapped in the bathroom—I can be stranded in my own home. (But if you were to tell me that I've never had the ability to organize and keep things in order, so it shouldn't be much different from normal, you would be right....)

When I think about how I met with such incredible good fortune and was allowed to write three books in this apartment, it gets a little hard to leave it.

This book, *Kieli III: Prisoners Bound for Another Planet,* is the third book in the *Kieli* series and is a continuation from volume two. If anyone read the prologue to this book and then went right to the afterword to see what was going on, I apologize for the misleading opening. This book is most definitely *Kieli*.

This time, the main setting is a mining town that has giant exhaust pipes spewing smoke, and that clings to the rocky wall of a fault. The ruins of a spaceship show up, too, so it's got a subtle sci-fi feel. Storywise, like the previous volumes, it's a story about a girl with a complicated personality and a man with a tiresome personality, getting together and being separated, and about a man, who's tired of living, being immature and getting kidnapped.

Rather than traveling, they're settled in one place, and the narrative has lost some of its episodic nature and gotten more like one long story, so it might have a somewhat different feel than the first two books, but I hope you enjoyed it.

Now then. Again, I have much gratitude for everyone who put forth effort to publish this book, and to my editor, who is so busy but still makes time for my whining and selfish requests. I'm still always running around in confusion, and I'm sorry for all the trouble I cause.

To Taue-san, who was kind enough to provide the wonderful, even more polished illustrations for this book: As usual, I'm sorry for being so fussy about all these weird machines like Harvey's prosthetic arm and the mad scientist's monocle. From the first volume, we've both said to each other, "Please don't abandon me!" but it's thanks to you that I've been able to write three volumes. Please don't abandon me...!

To my family, friends, and acquaintances: Once I've moved and settled down, I'll reform and practice better living habits....But I do wonder when things will ever settle down. I foresee having piles of cardboard boxes for at least six months.

To all the readers who sent letters to a novice author: I am truly very grateful as I read all of them. I pick them up when I visit the editorial department, and it's my secret joy to read them stealthily on the train ride home, but as I read, I can't help smiling bashfully or wryly, and I must be a very suspicious-looking passenger.

And I give my highest heartfelt thanks to you who are holding this book in your hands. I hope we get a chance to meet again.

I can hear the sound of the first train outside my window.
Soon I'll be saying good-bye to this five-story, rebar apartment, three buildings from the train tracks.